PENNY AND THE FARTHING

GAVIN THOMSON

MMXVIII

THIS BOOK BELONGS TO

_____

For Caroline

1   Gripp and Rocky!

2   Three Lions on a shirt!

3   A fuchsia pink painted hall!

4   Ju-don't do it like that, boys!

5   Pe-nny. Pe-nny. Pe-nny!

6   Instead of roaring, they shout GOAAAALLL!

7   There's no such thing as ghosts!

8   The Ceremony of the Liquorice!

9   The Old Gits, The Pretenders and The Newbies!

10   We true grits!

11   Smile like you mean it!

12   Roarrr!

13   Hello, Sis! Hello, Bro!

14   The Wars of The Bro-Sis!

15   You get pink!

16   To marry her sister's husband's brother!

17   Love, peace and harmony!

18   I'm a little hoarse!

19 Tattie tuna tombola!

20 Swaying trees!

21 Treason of the highest order!

22 A secret so great!

23 Air shoes!

24 Still no eye-deer!

25 Top-that!

26 Five turnips to four!

27 Weddings, funerals and coronations!

28 Knock, knock!

29 I hurry with Godspeed!

30 That's put a hammer in the works!

31 Fünf. Fünf. Fünf!

32 The great escape!

33 Operation *Three Lions* is go!

34 Let's wrestle!

35 Bye, Fenton. Bye, Filbert. Enjoy your evening!

36 Gripp and Rocky!

1
Gripp and Rocky!

"Tap. Tap. Tap."

"Tap. Tap. Tap," repeats the distinctive sound of bird beaks on the window pane. Penny rolls onto her side to face the window, scrunching her face to begin the pained process of awakening. She opens one eye and then the other, as she closes the first. It is early, and she has never been what you call *a morning person!*

"Tap. Tap. Tap."

"Alright, guys," acknowledges Penny, stretching and yawning before throwing back her duvet and revolving her legs to sit upright on the side of her bed, shouting, "I'm coming. Keep your hair on...I mean, keep your feathers on! Talk about the early bird catching the worm!"

Penny chuckles to herself, amusing herself with this daily routine of repeated banter and difficulty in rising from her sweet dreams. She grabs a gloss black tin box from her bedside cabinet, remembering how she has only herself to blame for encouraging this morning phenomenon while relishing this unique privilege and delight, as she ventures to the window and pulls back the curtains.

"Morning, Gripp. Morning, Rocky," greets Penny, immediately closing her eyes as the sunrise blasts through as if in desperate search of food and water. "How are you this morning?"

Penny lifts the antique metal lever and turns the equally old metal latch to open her window ajar. She unclips her tin box and takes out six liquorice sweets, placing three at the feet of each black raven, staring back at her as if to say, "Is that all! Don't be so stingy, Penny!" As they move their heads side to side robotically, their *hands* held behind their backs like Halloween apple bobbers grappling for the sweet reward.

"You should thank your lucky stars," declares Penny, closing her box ready for tomorrow's performance and talking to Gripp and Rocky as if they understand her every word, and she understands their every squawk and caw, continuing, "especially you, Gripp...*Greedy Gripp*, and you, Rocky...*Rocky Balboa*, stop fighting with Gripp. Be happy with yours. Otherwise, it's reduced rations for both of you tomorrow!"

Penny reminisces back to their first encounter, last Christmas, when she receives a jar of sweets from her Uncle and Aunt, much to the head-shaking of her Mum and Dad! Disliking the liquorice, tarnishing the otherwise fantastic assortment, she places them on her windowsill as a gesture of goodwill for any passing opportunist. Never in her wildest dreams did Penny expect two of the Tower of London ravens to be the eager recipients - how was she to know that besides a diet of mice, chicks, rats, assorted raw meats and blood-soaked biscuits that they would have a liking for liquorice! "It was you first, Rocky," remembers Penny, giving Rocky a favourable glance before turning to Gripp. "But you were only moments behind, Gripp, weren't you? It was two birds with one stone!" jokes Penny, mimicking their robotic head movements as she corrects herself. "I mean, two birds with one handful of discarded black and white liquorice!"

"Haw. Haw. Haw," Rocky and Gripp appear to laugh, only acting to encourage Penny's endless round of jokes and idioms, fuelled from her father's regularly added to repertoire.

Penny knows Gripp and Rocky by name after managing to dab red nail polish on Rocky and green nail polish on Gripp and observing them in their respective cages later in the day when the Tower's Ravenmaster calls them back for supper and *bedtime*.

"Are you gonna wish me luck?" asks Penny, treating Gripp and Rocky each to one more piece of liquorice. "It's my big judo competition today. Tower Hamlets v Greenwich."

"Brarrr. Brorrr," reply Grip and Rocky, repeating several times as if to emphasise their support. Penny, of course, reads this response as positive encouragement!

"Thank you, boys!" she responds, smiling and rubbing her eyes once more to put *sleep* to bed finally and welcome in this exciting new day, informing Gripp and Rocky, "If I win three bouts today, I'll win my brown belt. The first girl under eleven at the Tower Hamlets judo club to do so...ever!"

Gripp and Rocky bid their farewells, screeching and screaming before one by one, flying away awkwardly with their purposely clipped wings, appearing to fall to earth like dead weights rather than gliding gracefully back to their preferred position outside the Crown Jewels exit - the best place for rich pickings!

Penny leaves her window ajar to let the gentle breeze of fresh air circulate and replace snore-ridden morning breath. She glances around the room, wishing she could redecorate and adorn her walls with *pop* heroes and judo heroines - living in the Tower of London is an amazing experience, but it has its drawbacks.

Her father, Philip, shortened to *Phil*, a decorated Captain of the Royal Grenadiers, is now Chief Yeoman Warder, responsible for guarding and protecting the Crown Jewels. Penny often teases her Dad that he shouldn't be called a *Beefeater* but a *Veganeater*, given his dislike for meat and his quest to be as small a burden on the environment as he possibly can. Penny's Mum, Elizabeth, shortened to *Liz*, teases him further by saying that a *Veganeater* makes him sound like he eats vegans, which Liz finds extremely funny, given her opposing view. Penny is indifferent. It's all food for thought!

The other Yeomen refer to the three of them as the *Royal Family* - Liz, Phil and Lady Penelope!

Penelope Gladys Woodville is Penny's full name. She is ten years old and attends the local primary school, half a mile's walk due east. Her hair is golden, shoulder-length and extremely thick, making it impossible to brush and manage. Penny refuses to tie it back and is pleased to parade her *bed head* for all to see, likening herself to a tomboy more likely to get her hands dirty than to sit back in subdued silence. She has blue eyes and freckles. Her natural beauty is lost on her as she smiles with an overcrowded and twisted grin, and she favours sportswear over some dress or trousers and a top. Her longing for a sibling vanished when they moved to the Tower, which provides easy access and proximity to other children her age. That said, Penny is content to be alone and explore her imagination.

Phil is a stickler for routine and order. His idea of discipline may be overstated in today's world, but Penny knows the boundaries and the lines she must never cross. Ironically, she finds it empowering and in no way inhibitive. Praise has a greater impact and reprimands act as a catalyst for improvement rather than a deterrent. Manners and respect make perfect sense, especially growing up in the surroundings of an almost thousand-year-old legacy, riddled with stories of darker and more troublesome times, but enduring to represent resilience, constancy and social responsibility, romanticised by mythical tales of superstition and legends of historical significance. Howls of the executed *cry out* when the wind blows in a particular direction, and at least six ravens must remain captive within the confines of the grounds to avert disaster to the *kingdom* and keep the Tower from *falling*, contrary to the wishes of the resident astronomer before moving the observatory to Greenwich.

Liz is the antithesis of Phil. They are a perfect example where opposites attract. Phil is tall, dark and rugged. Liz is petite, blond and dainty. Phil is a disciplinarian. Liz is a libertarian. Phil dresses in uniform and runs to clockwork. Liz dresses in fashionable and colourful clothes and wears no watch even though she has an uncanny reputation for never being late. Phil is calm and understated. Liz is loud and larger than life. Phil joins the army and is now a Yeoman. Liz is a travel photographer before placing her career on hold to raise Penny. However, she is never seen without her trusty *Nikon*, snapping and recording every minute detail of their everyday life. Liz works part-time at the Tower.

Phil and Liz met at a mutual friend's wedding, and their love blossomed immediately. They are a match made in heaven. Penny loves hearing their courtship stories and their battle to conquer distance and different worlds.

After washing and brushing her teeth, Penny puts on her favourite orange tracksuit, embroidered with a large blue letter P on the back, a pair of silver and white trainers and makes her way downstairs to join Liz and Phil for breakfast.

2
Three Lions on a shirt!

"Cup of tea?" Phil asks Penny as she enters the kitchen and pulls up a seat at the breakfast table laden with various cereals, jams and essential condiments.

"Can I have a chai latte?" requests Penny, reaching for the bran flakes, smiling and raising her eyebrows, and begging her Dad with fluttered eyelashes. Liz sips her coffee with her back turned to Phil and gives Penny a look of support, gritting her teeth and tensing her mouth with wide eyes, awaiting Phil's response.

"A what?" replies Phil, replacing the freshly filled kettle on its base and flicking the switch.

"A chai latte!" repeats Penny, pointing to the brand-new chai tea box next to the Tower of London tin housing Phil's favourite breakfast brew, adding, "It's black tea blended with oriental spices...hot frothy milk, and finished with a pinch of cinnamon."

"Sounds like a lot of fuss for a morning drink," dismisses Phil, shaking his head and sighing deeply, continuing. "When we were marooned in the desert, awaiting assistance to retrieve us from behind enemy lines - hot water poured over a single teabag shared between six of us...with neither milk nor sugar was the simple taste of heaven..."

"...and that's why Penny can have a chai latte," interjects Liz, making her way to the fridge to fetch the milk and kissing Phil gently on the cheek as she passes. "Because soldiers like you fight for and defend our freedom...the freedom to make these very choices, however insignificant they might seem."

Phil nods and softens, smiling at Penny and Liz in turn. He is wearing his regular Yeoman uniform trousers - black with a thin red side stripe and his mirror-polished boots. Still, instead of his regular white undershirt pending his black and red tunic, hanging behind the kitchen door, Phil is wearing an England football shirt.

"Why the England shirt, Daddy?" enquires Penny as she blows hard on her chai latte, marvelling at the swirling milk patterns and thinking how much they resemble an infinity of hearts.

"We're through to the Second Round!" replies Phil, puffing his chest out and displaying the Three Lions crest with pride, enthusing, "England are playing Wales today in the World Cup."

"Not football!" exclaims Liz, joking as she unzips her top to reveal her England shirt, cheering, "C'mon, England! C'mon, England! You can beat Wales!"

"I thought you said England had no chance," points out Penny, embarrassed by her parents standing in the kitchen and singing *Three Lions* at the top of their voices.

"We did," replies Phil as he and Liz sing in unison, "*It's coming home, it's coming home, football's coming home!*"

"It's the new manager," informs Liz, finishing the song and smiling at Phil, both saying, "I love that song, but let's not get carried away. It's too early to start believing!"

"Yeah!" continues Phil, pressing his hands together in prayer and closing his eyes to look heavenwards, adding, "He's taken a young team - a young team with no expectations on them, and created a fearless team..."

"...united them as a team rather than a bunch of individuals, now playing with passion and hunger," contributes Liz, smiling like a little girl at Penny, making Penny reflect how behind the façade of responsibility, adults are just grown-up kids!

"We've got a great defence, a goalkeeper who's playing out of his skin, a midfield that's running circles around the opposition and a front line that can hit them in from outside the box or head them in at the near post," excites Phil, placing his right hand on his England badge.

"And don't forget the set pieces, Darling," adds Liz, downing the last few drops of her coffee and munching her final piece of toast, "We've scored more goals from free-kicks and corners than we've ever done before."

"That's right, Darling," agrees Phil, nodding vehemently, "and let's not forget the centre-half with that long throw. It's like we get a corner every time the opposition knocks the ball out in their own half!"

Penny stares at the England crest with intrigue before asking, "Why the *three lions*, and what do the *ten red roses* stand for?"

Liz looks at Phil, hoping he has the answer. "The Three Lions are the royal crest for the Plantagenets, dating back to kings like Richard the First, the Lionheart in the thirteenth century...to lead armies into battle," answers Phil, looking at his badge upside down, continuing. "It's not certain, but the red roses represent the Wars of the Roses - thirty years of English Civil War in the fifteenth century when Richard of York, of the House of York and the white rose, rebelled against King Henry the Sixth, of the House of Lancaster and the red rose, waging bloody battles but

14

taking risks resulting in his death, and passing the buck to his son who eventually defeats Henry the Sixth to become Edward the Fourth. Then Henry the Sixth reclaims the throne with the help of a wealthy landowner, the Earl of Warwick, only to lose it again to Edward, who then dies suddenly to be succeeded by his twelve-year-old son, Edward the Fifth, who only reigns for seventy-eight days before his uncle, Richard of Gloucester, imprisons him in the Tower, along with his nine-year-old brother, Richard - *the Princes in the Tower*, to become Richard the Third after the Princes are denounced and mysteriously disappear. Then two years later, Richard the Third is defeated at the Battle of Bosworth Field by another Henry, a loose relative of Henry the Sixth who becomes Henry the Seventh, putting an end to the Plantagenets, the Wars of the Roses with his marriage to Elizabeth - Edward the Fifth's sister, and begins the dynasty of the Tudors!"

"So, the *Three Lions* crest represents a call to battle?" summarises Penny, fascinated by Phil's succinct description.

"That's right, Penny," agrees Phil, contemplating its significance for the first time, adding, "although the England football team had to seek permission to use the crest, given its royal heritage. The rugby team adopts a red rose, but the cricket team also has three lions, funnily enough. It probably best sums up the complications of English history!"

"The Scots have a single lion for football and the thistle for rugby," contributes Liz, demonstrating her keen sporting knowledge, "while the Welsh have the dragon for football and the Prince of Wales feathers for rugby!"

"What happened to the Princes in the Tower?" asks Penny, excited by their connection to her home - the Tower.

15

"There are many theories," begins Phil, delighting in Penny's interest, "but none are proven. Some say it was Richard the Third - others say it was his sidekick, the Duke of Buckingham. While some say It was Henry the Seventh, and others say they died of natural causes...although Richard the Third would have told everyone if that was the case. And some say they escaped to declare their rights to the throne later. It's a complete mystery."

"Weren't skeletons found during King Charles the Second's reign?" asks Liz, recalling information from the Tower tour.

"That's right," confirms Phil, nodding before shaking his head. "If those skeletons belong to the Princes, and that's a big *IF*, it makes the escape theory unlikely, but it doesn't resolve who killed them or how they died. They were imprisoned on the second floor on the right-hand side of the Tower as you look towards the river."

"So, not the Bloody Tower?" enquires Penny, pointing towards the window.

"That was before they were imprisoned, Darling," says Liz, looking at her watch, exclaiming, "Look at the time! Phil, you need to get to work, and Penny, we need to get to the water bus in twenty minutes. So, get your judo kit together while I clear up."

"Good luck today, Penny," shouts Phil as he puts on his red tunic, embellished with chest medals and a gold chevroned sleeve badge denoting his Chief Yeoman position. He grabs his hat, kisses Liz and opens the front door, adding, "I wish I could be there to see you get your brown belt, but I look forward to hearing all about it when you come to the Yeoman Warders Club for the England-Wales game at six o'clock. We're shutting the Tower of London to the public at five-thirty in preparation! Bye!"

16

3
A fuchsia pink painted hall!

Penny knocks three times next door. Within seconds, the door swings open to reveal two beaming boys jostling to exit first. They are brothers and Penny's best friends away from school. Ted is older at twelve, and Rick is younger at nine. They look like brothers, and in their boyish innocence, they bear a distinct resemblance to Penny - both boys sporting long golden hair, blue eyes and freckles. Many think they are all related, which amuses them. They often perpetuate this by referring to each other as *Sis* or *Bro,* and Penny and Ted, being identical in height, sometimes mimic twins, rehearsing and repeating sentences simultaneously to further freak out the uninformed. Ted and Rick's father, John, is another Yeoman. Their mother, Beth, is an art historian, expert in every detail of the Tower and responsible for a team of twelve to conduct tours all day, every day for the never-ending queue of fascinated visitors. John and Beth Suffolk are Phil and Liz's best friends.

"Watcha, Penny," greets Ted, winning the race to the front step and leaving Rick to pull the door closed before spying Liz, patiently standing a few metres down the lane. "Good morning, Mrs Woodville."

"Yes, good morning, Mrs Woodville," adds Rick, politely and standing alongside his brother. Ted and Rick look more dishevelled than other boys with an ex-military parent, but their manners are impeccable. Beth insists on long hair, contrary to the rigid dress codes of the armed services, and they like it - it sets them apart...despite being mistaken for girls occasionally!

"Morning, Ted. Morning, Rick," replies Liz, holding what appears to be a beach bag and turning to lead the way to the water bus. "Have you got everything?"

"Yes, Mrs Woodville," reply Ted and Rick in unison, looking at each other for confirmation.

"Let me get a photo of the three of you," requests Liz, gesturing for Penny, Ted and Rick to face her when they reach the White Tower as a backdrop and instructing. "Smile like you mean in it. One, two, three, cheese!"

"Cheeeeese!" ventriloquism Penny, Ted and Rick with forced smiles and raised thumbs.

"Super," thanks Liz, snapping five shots and examining the results in her camera's rear display. "Right. Let's get to Greenwich."

"It's England v Wales today," says Penny, glancing at her mother with a wry smile, adding, "The Second Round of the World Cup."

"We know," reply Ted and Rick, unzipping their tracksuit tops to reveal England shirts, both chanting, *"Three Lions on a shirt!"*

"Dad says they're showing the match at the Yeoman Warders Club at six," continues Penny, looking at Ted and then Rick, as she accompanies them behind Liz like an advancing midfield attack. "Are you gonna watch?"

"Absolutely!" Ted and Rick exclaim before Ted adds, "Three-one to England!" and Rick follows with, "Three-two to England!"

Liz leads them diagonally across Tower Green, past the vacant Raven cages and the Bloody Tower, along Water Lane and through the main entrance to take a left turn down towards the river. Penny, Ted and Rick follow in autopilot, chatting without a care in the world and wearing their judo kit black backpacks.

They wait at the Tower Millennium Pier, observing six minutes for the next *Greenwich Pier* water bus. Liz takes another few photos, this time placing Tower Bridge as the backdrop and directing Penny and Ted to replicate the opening left and right bascules while Rick makes his best impression of a high-masted clipper. Initial awkwardness is soon replaced with bellyaching laughter. So much so - even Liz must compose herself to avoid camera wobble!

Liz flashes her *privilege pass* to the conductor. She escorts the children onto the water bus, smiling to herself as Penny and Ted pay her no attention and drag Rick to the outside deck, leaving her to follow like an unwanted chaperone of bygone courtship.

The water bus gurgles and splutters like an overloaded washing machine and pulls away from the pier before surfing on the out-flowing tidal Thames water with the motion and quietness of a modern dishwasher.

Liz marvels at the engineering masterpiece as they pass under Tower Bridge - lost on Penny, Ted and Rick...otherwise engaged with taking *selfies* on Ted's new phone, trying their best to out-pout each other!

Liz takes a photo of them without their knowledge, delighting in their dramatic confidence, usually dragged out under duress or with coy resistance.

"*Next stop. Canary Wharf,*" informs the Tannoy with better than usual electronic diction and added reassurance, "*Final Destination. Greenwich Pier.*"

"Look, kids," enthuses Liz, pointing to the post-modern architecture of Canary Wharf Tower and its surrounding hotchpotch of debatable contributions. "It's Canary Wharf!"

Penny, Ted and Rick pause to stare in the direction of Liz's finger only to disappoint Liz with unimpressed grimaces. It's as if she'd asked them to smell fresh manure!

"Ah, Mum!" moans Penny, embarrassed by Liz's interruption, "They're just office blocks!"

Liz says nothing, snapping away for her personal indulgence.

The water bus edges its way down the Isle of Dogs, revealing layers of urban evolution like a sea vessel sailing along the Dorset Jurassic Coast and observing prehistoric rock formations.

The water bus gurgles and splutters again as it repels water to park conveniently against Greenwich Pier. Liz makes sure everyone has everything, and they disembark.

They walk inland admiring The Cutty Sark and The Gypsy Moth, commenting on the risks of sailing around the world.

"Now, let me see where we need to go," begins Liz, retrieving her phone and scrolling through her messages. "I'm sure there was an email from your judo instructor, Mr Hastings...now, where is it?" she continues rhetorically.

"I'll text my Mum," offers Ted, finger typing his message before Liz can respond, informing her. "There. It's gone!"

"Don't bother your Mum at work," says Liz, shaking her head and becoming annoyed that she can't find Mr Hastings' email.

"Painted Hall in Greenwich," reads Ted as he types back in full rather than text-speech. *Thank you* and *see you later. Ted x.*

"That rings a bell from Mr Hastings' email," replies Liz, replacing the phone in her pocket.

"I hope it's better than *our* painted hall!" remarks Rick.

"Yeah!" adds Penny, "Whoever thought it was a good idea to paint our hall in fuchsia pink needs their head examining."

"Apparently, one of the senior members is a *painter and decorator,* and he had a job lot left over from one of his contracts, and he offered to do it for free," defends Liz, hopelessly!

"But pink!" exclaims Ted, "Why did it have to be *fuchsia* pink!?"

The Tower Hamlets Judo club meets in a community hall attached to the back of one of the local pubs, appropriately called *The Wrestler.* It has no airs and graces, but it does the job and keeps the weekly subs modest and affordable.

"Excuse me, sir," Liz asks a traffic warden as he taps out a ticket for some poor offender, "We're looking for a painted hall."

"You mean, *The Painted Hall!*" replies the warden, pointing towards the Old Royal Naval College, "You'll find it in there."

Liz thanks the warden and crosses the road with Penny, Ted and Rick. They find the entrance to The Old Royal Navy College and follow the temporary signs marked *Judo Competition.* They say nothing as they wander the halls - everyone dwarfed by the scale and humbled by the grandeur and opulence. Then without warning, they enter the soaring domed Vestibule, and their eyes stumble into the Lower Hall and beyond into the Upper Hall.

Their jaws drop as they stand in stunned silence, fixated on the ceiling, and wrestle for words of comparison with their own *painted hall!*

21

4

Ju-don't do it like that, boys!

Will Hastings, the Tower Hamlets Junior Judo Coach, ushers Liz, Penny, Ted and Rick up the full-width staircase and into the Lower Hall. Will is in his early fifties with short greying hair and a muscular physique - a true gentleman, exuding charm and tranquillity. "Hi, Penny...Ted...Rick," he welcomes, rubbing his hands as if it were the middle of winter instead of the middle of June, continuing. "Well done for making it in good time. What do you think of the venue, ...knockout...yes!?"

"This is unbelievable," answers Liz, stepping forward with an outstretched hand. "Hi, Mr Hastings. Liz...Liz Woodville. Penny's Mum."

"Hi, Liz. Call me, Will," he replies, shaking her hand slightly too hard for comfort, apologising. "Sorry. I don't know my own strength, sometimes!"

"Beats the pink hall at The Wrestler!" jokes Liz, changing the subject and gesturing to the painted masterpieces.

"You betcha!" acknowledges Will, pointing directly upwards. "I've been told that this Lower Hall ceiling celebrates the *Triumph of Peace and Liberty over Tyranny* with King William and Queen Mary *standing* on King Louis the Fourteenth of France!"

"Fascinating," nods Liz, ensuring that Penny, Ted and Rick are parties to Will's description.

"And The Upper Hall ceiling has Queen Anne and hubby, Prince George of Denmark, next to depictions of Europe, Asia, America and Africa, and the coats of arms of England, Scotland, France

22

and Ireland," Will continues as he points to The Upper Hall and motions left with his right hand to complete his description. "And The West Wall celebrates George the First and the Hanoverians, reinforcing messages of peace and prosperity and naval supremacy."

"Wow!" remarks Liz, smiling at Will, "You should get a job here...as a guide!"

"I was so impressed by the location," responds Will, blushing slightly, "I had to find out about it!"

"Absolutely!" agrees Liz, snapping a few shots with her camera, "You're talking to people who live in the Tower of London!"

Penny, Ted and Rick have seen enough of the paintings and lower their gaze to the competition set-up. The Lower Hall has three rows of white coloured chairs nearside with a central aisle leading to a full-width black tatami mat construction square edging a bright orange contest area and a repeat of three rows of red coloured chairs farside again with a central aisle. Narrow walkways run down each side of the floor to ceiling windows fitted with white blinds to neutralise the sunlight.

On the face of it, the set-up resembles every other set-up they've been to, but somehow this unique setting increases its impact and significance. Penny's heart skips a beat as butterflies flap their wings wildly against her stomach lining. The opposing red and white chairs make her think back to the breakfast conversation and the talk about the Wars of The Roses. She thanks her lucky stars that no weapons are allowed today!

Ted breaks this reflection. "Where do we get changed, Mr Hastings?"

Will directs them back downstairs towards the entrance where two rooms have been turned into changing rooms - *red* is Tower Hamlets, and *white* is Greenwich.

By ten to eleven, the Lower Hall is transformed into the hustle and bustle of two opposing teams and their supporters, encamping each side like Members of Parliament ready to jeer each other down. Penny, Ted and Rick sit in the front row of the red seats alongside their teammates. They are wearing their red competition *judogi* uniform emblazoned on the back with the Tower Hamlets Judo Club logo and wearing a coloured *obi* belt. Ted wears a brown belt, Penny a blue belt and Rick a green belt. Greenwich is wearing white judogi.

Liz sits behind. An organiser reprimands her for taking photographs. Now she must rely on the official photographer's point of view...and pay the price for it!

Will walks up and down with clipboard in hand. He is wearing his teaching judogi - black *uwagi* jacket and *zubon* trousers with a *kuro obi* black belt. His younger opposite number, Henry Buckingham - nicknamed Duke, is smaller and portlier with wavy red hair and wearing yellow judogi with a kuro obi. Will and Duke know each other of old and meet in the middle to shake hands.

"Hi, Will," begins Duke, shaking hands and quipping. "Are you ready to do *battle*, Hastings!?"

"Hi, Duke," replies Will, squeezing tighter and tighter. "We are ready to *conquer*...if that's what you mean!" then softening to exchange pleasantries, "How's Kathy and the pregnancy?"

Will and Duke continue their banter until the referee, dressed in a blue blazer, grey slacks, and a white shirt with a green tie, comes over to commence proceedings. "Morning, Gentlemen," he starts, standing to their side. "My name is Tony Rivers. I want a clean competition, and I will disqualify any opponent if the support becomes unruly. Do we understand each other?" Will and Duke nod before bowing and returning to their respective sides. An adjudicator bangs the gong for an eleven o'clock start.

The morning session comprises a Round Robin. Only brown, blue, and green belt grades are competing. Each belt grade has three male or female players on each side, playing each other in a three-minute contest and scoring for *throwing, pinning* or achieving *a submission*. After lunch, the matched players from each side play each other again in a five to ten-minute contest, depending on their level. The winners score points for their team. The team with the most points receives the gold-plated trophy!

Incidentally, if Penny wins three contests, she will also achieve the next grade - a brown belt. Ted and Rick haven't earned enough points in the season to be in this position.

The Round Robin sounds like a logistical nightmare, but each player receives three contest numbers totalling twenty-seven contests, playing one belt grade after another. Rick has contest numbers, one, thirteen and twenty-nine, Penny has contest numbers five, eleven and seventeen, and Ted has contest numbers, nine, twenty-one and twenty-seven. A flip board announces each contest, and incredulously, like clockwork, it takes one hundred and eight minutes, allowing for one minute between contests!

They each win their first contest. Rick, two-one. Penny, three-nil. Ted, one-nil.

Penny loses her second contest, two-three. Rick wins his second contest, three-two. Ted is yet to fight before Penny wins her third and final contest, three-two.

Will offers congratulations or commiserations, following immediately with words of encouragement and pats on the back. Duke is a mirror image, albeit a distorted one!

Liz supplies a steady stream of refreshments from her beach bag. She acts as *masseuse and motivator* between contests, occasionally receiving a stern look from the referee for her over-exuberant cheering during each contest!

Rick loses his third contest, one-three. Ted draws his second contest but wins his third contest, two-one. It is lunchtime. They will announce the order of afternoon play when they reconvene.

Liz suggests a picnic outside. Penny, Ted, Rick and Liz exit the Old Royal Naval college into Greenwich Park to catch the bright red Time Ball rise halfway on the observatory spire at five minutes to one. They stop to ensure they do not miss the Time Ball rise to the top at two minutes to, then drop like a bingo ball to denote one o'clock precisely.

"That's like me..." boasts Ted, playfully throwing Rick over his right leg to the ground, "...flooring my last opponent!"

"Ju-don't do it like that, boys!" shouts Penny, grabbing Ted by his uwagi, tipping him backwards to confuse his sense of balance, then pulling him forward while simultaneously twisting him around her body to bring him to the ground and staring back at her with dented pride!

5
Pe-nny. Pe-nny. Pe-nny!

Just as Penny releases her grip, Ted grabs her uwagi, and with one swift movement, he wraps his right leg around her ankles and pulls Penny to the ground beside him.

"Ahhh!" screams Penny, forcing Ted to release, "My ankle!"

"That's enough, you three!" declares Liz, shaking out the picnic blanket and lowering it to the ground as if she were making a bed. "It'll end in tears, and someone'll get hurt."

"Yes. Me!" exclaims Penny, sitting up to grab her ankle, still trapped in between Ted's legs. "I think it's twisted."

"What do you mean?" questions Ted, rolling away and sitting up.

Rick comes over and offers Penny his hand. Penny grabs hold, and after some toing and froing and Rick almost sitting, Penny stands up to discover she cannot put any weight on her ankle. Liz unravels a selection of homemade sandwiches, unaware of the severity. "OMG!" cries Penny, limping forwards then grabbing Rick as a crutch. "I can't walk."

"Let me look," offers Liz, observing Penny in pain.

"Is it OK?" enquires Ted sheepishly, realising that he has taken things too far.

"Does that hurt?" asks Liz as she pushes Penny's foot up and down, then left and right.

"Yep!" answers Penny, grimacing then giving Ted daggers, "I won't be able to fight this afternoon and get my brown belt."

"I suggest you have some lunch and rest it," suggests Liz, rubbing Penny's ankle. "If we were at home, we could wrap some ice around it or some frozen peas."

"Or use the *magic sponge!*" says Rick, trying to lighten the situation, "Like footballers use in the World Cup!"

"I wish," declares Penny, sighing deeply and shaking her head with pursed lips.

"I'm really sorry, Penny," apologises Ted, resting on the blanket beside her. "It was an accident. Promise."

"Absolutely!" reassures Liz, smiling at Ted. "Accidents happen. It was no one's fault or both your fault...depending on how you look at it. Let's eat. Egg mayonnaise or ham and cheese?"

After food, Liz, Ted and Rick play frisbee while Penny remains on the blanket with her ankle raised on the beach bag.

"Right. It's quarter to two," Liz asks a passer-by, "I think we should be getting back."

Liz helps up Penny while Ted and Rick stand on either side to provide support. Liz packs everything away, and they return to the Old Royal Naval College. Penny is determined to work through the pain and carry on, as usual, limping less and less as they reach the Lower Hall to read with intrigue the Round Robin results and this afternoon's timetable.

"I came top of my group!" declares Rick, proudly as he consults the afternoon timetable. "I have to contest my third opponent, again...the one who beat me earlier!"

"Where did you come, Penny?" enquires Ted before he reveals his results.

"I came second," says Penny, slightly disappointed, "and like Rick, I have to contest the person who beat me - my second opponent. What about you, Ted?"

"I came first," replies Ted, trying to hide his joy before rubbing it in further, "and I get to contest my first opponent, whom I beat...just!"

They return to their seats and chat to Will about tactics before Tony reappears to resume proceedings. "Firstly, may I say how well you all contested this morning, and thank you for making everything run so smoothly. This afternoon, we have nine contests. Three five-minute contests for green belts, three seven-minute contests for blue belts and three ten-minute contests for brown belts. May I remind everyone that the Round Robin points will be added in the event of a draw? As you will see from the board, Greenwich leads Tower Hamlets by one point - fourteen points to thirteen. It couldn't be more evenly matched. To make it more exciting, the afternoon order will be drawn out of a hat. So, without further ado, let the contests begin!"

The adjudicator bangs the gong at two o'clock.

The second brown belt pair contest first - two boys grunting and groaning and determined to gain a submission. Tower Hamlets wins five-four and secures a point. The third brown belt pair contests next. Greenwich wins six-three and secures a point. The third blue belt pair contests next. Two evenly matched girls fight hammer and tongs until Tower Hamlets pins Greenwich in the last ten seconds to win four-three and secure another point. Then the second green belt pair contest, initially warned for delaying tactics, eventually seeing Greenwich win three-two to acquire another point. It's two-two after four matches. Rick is next.

"C'mon, Rick," encourage Ted, Penny and Liz with clenched fists, adding, "you can do it!"

Rick knows his opponent has the advantage by beating him earlier, but he changes tack to avoid his previous errors and, after five hard-fought minutes, secures a two-two draw and shares the point. Rick is delighted and sits down to cheers - it feels more like a win not to lose! Greenwich cheer Rick's opponent, but Penny senses disappointment in their tone.

The first blue belt contest ends with Tower Hamlets securing a point with a two-one win, followed by the third green belt pair contesting a three-two win and a point for Greenwich.

It is three and a half points each after seven matches. Will it be Penny or Ted to contest next? Ted's name is called. He jumps to his feet like a jack-in-a-box, smacking his arms and beating his chest to psyche himself. He knows his team needs a win.

"Te-ed. Te-ed," cheer Tower Hamlets, battling to be heard over Greenwich, cheering, "E-ddy. E-ddy."

Somehow, Ted's opponent emerges like another player making them even at three-three after five minutes with two minutes remaining. Another minute passes. Then Eddy moves right, sending Ted off-balance, throwing Ted over his left leg to the floor and landing on Ted to incapacitate him under his now heavily panting body and gain a four-three advantage. Twenty seconds remain, and Ted is staring defeat in the face. He replicates his earlier throw on Penny, wrapping his legs around Eddy's ankles and pulling him down to secure another point. The contest ends in a four-four draw and halves the point.

It is now four points, all with one contest to go - Penny's! A draw or loss will hand victory to Greenwich. Penny must win. She congratulates Ted - returning red-faced and dripping in sweat.

"You can do it, Penny," Ted whispers in her ear. "Bring it home!" Penny ignores her ankle pain and stands opposite her opponent - the boy who beat her earlier. Humphrey. Every time Penny goes to throw Humphrey, her ankle gives way, making it impossible to score in the first three minutes. Humphrey smells her weakness and keeps wrapping his right leg around her left leg, trying to make it buckle under Penny's weight. Penny spends all her time defending rather than attacking. Thirty seconds remain, and there is still no score.

The crowd is going mad. "Pe-nny. Pe-nny," screams Tower Hamlets. "Hum-phrey. Hum-phrey," bellows Greenwich, sensing a draw and a win by default!

Penny feigns weakness, making Humphrey push, pulling him forwards and off-balance. Penny sits down and draws her knees up to support Humphrey. Then with both hands on his uwagi, she rocks backwards, thrusting her arms above her head and launching Humphrey into a forward roll as she lifts her knees, tumbling him onto his back. Penny and Humphrey lie on the tatami - their heads touching...both looking at Tony for a decision.

Tony looks at Penny then Humphrey then points to Penny, just as the gong goes to end the contest and the competition.

Penny wins the point. Tower Hamlets wins the competition, running onto the tatami like pitch-invading football fans, and lifts Penny into the air, chanting, "Pe-nny. Pe-nny. Pe-nny!"

6

Instead of roaring, they shout GOAAAALLL!

Penny, Ted, Rick and Liz sit on the return water bus - this time happy to find a place inside and recharge. Penny changed back into her tracksuit bottoms but kept on her uwagi so that she can show off her new belt - brown and double-tied!

Will anticipated three wins for Penny and presented her with the brown belt moments after the fracas of victory.

Liz has camera withdrawal symptoms and cannot stop snapping away, recording the euphoria of success for posterity and to email everyone later.

Penny, Ted and Rick relive every minute and every minute detail, embellishing and exaggerating like an angler describing *the fish that got away*. As they approach Tower Bridge, the conversation turns from judo to football. Ted and Rick take off their tracksuit tops to display their England shirts, followed shortly by Liz.

"I wish I had an England shirt," moans Penny, staring enviously at the other three. "To watch the match like a real fan."

"We'll get you one next week, Penny," happily offers Liz.

"You can borrow my other England shirt," offers Ted, seeing Penny's face light up. "The redshirt - England's second shirt."

"That's fantastic!" excites Penny, enjoying the thought of a redshirt to match her red uwagi.

"It's the least I can do," says Ted with a guilty smile, "after hurting your ankle."

Penny says nothing and gives a wry smile. Her ankle is still sore.

"You better hurry," directs Liz, spying the time on the water bus clock as they pull into Tower Millennium pier, "it's gone half-past five, and the match starts at six."

Liz shows her identity pass to one of the Queen's Guard, smartly dressed in a red tunic and a Busby bearskin hat and holding a rifle to his shoulder. She knocks on the large wooden entrance to get one of the Yeomen to let them in. Liz whispers the new daily password. Her friend, Brian, who has drawn the short straw to remain at the gate during the match, makes a joke about the password being incorrect before smiling and allowing Liz, Penny, Ted and Rick to enter and return home.

They walk quickly, or in Penny's case, limp like a wounded soldier past the occupied raven cages. Penny shouts *hello* to Gripp and Rocky and *see you in the morning* as they pass the White Tower and the Crown Jewels to arrive at Ted and Rick's house. Beth opens the door and quizzes Liz and Penny all about the judo competition while Ted and Rick hurry indoors to drop off their gear and return with Penny's red England shirt.

Beth, Ted and Rick wait outside while Liz drops off the beach bag, and Penny runs upstairs to deposit her backpack and change into the England shirt. It smells of Ted, but there is no time to be fussy! She puts on her uwagi to proudly display her brown belt and limps downstairs to rejoin everyone.

"I got you kids one of these from the gift shop," begins Beth as she delves into a Tower of London plastic bag to retrieve three *lion* toy headgear, "They're World Cup specials," she continues as Penny, Ted and Rick thank her and place them on their heads. "Instead of roaring, they shout GOAAAALLL!"

Penny, Ted and Rick are in hysterics as they look at each other with large lion noses, fat furry ears and long black whiskers, continually pressing the noses to roar *GOAAALLL!*

"Well done, Beth," applauds Liz, snapping another photo. "They're great! I wish we all had one!"

Liz and Beth follow the *three lions* to the Yeoman Warders Club and into a room laid out with rows of seats and a central aisle and the largest television screen Penny has ever seen.

The room seems naturally split into white England supporters on the left and red Wales supporters on the right! Penny feels awkward sitting in red on the left side but soon realises that there are more red England shirts encamped on the Wales side!

Penny, Ted and Rick spot their friends wearing red Wales shirts and similar *red dragon* toy headgear. They all press their noses simultaneously to make the whole room laugh at three lions and three dragons roaring GOAAAALLL.

"Thank goodness the dragons don't spit fire!" shouts one of the Yeomen, adding to the amusement.

Everyone stands for the National anthems. The English supporters outnumber the Wales supporters, but the Wales supporters have a distinct choral advantage!

"Well done today, guys," congratulates Phil, handing Penny, Ted and Rick a *St. Clement* orange and lemon drink, "I heard you kicked Greenwich butt!"

"Oh, Dad!" winces Penny, embarrassed by Phil's attempt to be *in with the kids!*

"And huge congratulations to you, Penny, on your brown belt," continues Phil, ignoring Penny's embarrassment, "I wish I could've been there, but Mum told me all about it, and I've seen some photos. I'm so proud of you!"

"Thanks, Dad," replies Penny, straw-sipping her drink, adding, "I've hurt my ankle."

"Yes, I heard," concerns Phil, "I'm sure it'll be much better in the morning."

"I hope so," wishes Penny, nodding at Phil.

"You *three lions* enjoy the match," concludes Phil as he returns to the back of the room, cheering, "C'mon, England!"

The first half is excruciating - near miss after near miss...on both sides!

With drinks replenished, everyone settles down for the second half. The enthusiasm of the first half has waned slightly. Then out of nowhere, the Wales defence robs the ball and catch England with a counter-attack, passing the ball up the right-wing as their strikers steam forward like bats out of hell, shimmying left and right to wrong-foot the England defence.

"C'mon, Wales," shout the Wales supporters.

"Get back, England," scream the England supporters.

The Wales winger floats a fantastic ball to the far post. The England goalkeeper is too far forwards and can only watch in vain as the Wales striker jumps into the air like a rugby line-out lock to head the ball into the back of the England net. It is one-nil to Wales. The Wales supporters go berserk with dragons roaring GOAAAALLL. The England supporters are stunned and silent!

Ten minutes later, Wales miskick the ball upfield, slicing it into the crowd. England's talisman collects the ball, and before Wales can regroup, he throws the longest throw of his life to fall into the five-yard box for the English *number nine* to flick it towards the far post and onto the end of the outstretched foot of the *number seven*. GOAAAALLL!

No one wants extra time, but the match looks like it is heading that way. Both teams seem happy to play down the clock. Then a stupid tackle by the Wales midfield hands England a free-kick thirty yards out. Three England players huddle around the ball while their teammates jostle for position. Even the England goalkeeper enters the array. The referee blows his whistle. The first England player is a decoy, running through the ball. The second player moves right as if to accept a pass. The third player contacts the ball with the *sweet spot* of his boot, and *banana kicks* the ball through the air and past every player, now spectators to the inevitable GOAAAALLL. England win two-one!

The Yeoman Warders Club erupts into amplified emotions of joy. Liz and Phil are ecstatic, hugging and jumping up and down - John and Beth doing the same! Penny, Ted, and Rick run around the room, roaring GOAAAALLL, rubbing Wales faces in defeat.

The whistle blows for full time. The England supporters cannot believe they are through to the quarter-finals. This achievement does not happen to England - at least, not for a very long time! The Wales supporters console themselves with a World Cup exit to the goal of the tournament so far.

The sausage rolls and egg sandwiches flow. Everyone is hungry!

7
There's no such thing as ghosts!

At nine-thirty, Phil comes over to Penny, Ted and Rick, interrupting their funny photo snaps and uploads to social media, "It's time you were in bed. Mum will take you back. I need to go and lock the gates."

"Do you mean the Ceremony of the Keys?" enquires Ted, knowing that this happens twice a day every day, come rain or shine.

"Can we come?" asks Penny before Phil can answer Ted.

Phil hesitates for a moment, reflecting on the countless times he's performed the Ceremony. "Seeing as England are through to the quarters," he begins, watching Penny, Ted and Rick sit upright and suppress smiles, "I don't see why not!"

"Brilliant, Dad!" thanks Penny, releasing her smile to accompany Ted and Rick's beaming grins.

"But you must stand well back," instructs Phil, beginning to have second thoughts, "and not make a single sound!"

Penny, Ted and Rick inform Liz, Beth and John and follow Phil towards the front gates, taking the same diagonal shortcut past the White Tower, the sleeping ravens and along Water Lane, where Phil leaves them briefly to prepare.

At precisely seven minutes to ten, Phil emerges from the Byward Tower, wearing his traditional red Watch Coat and Tudor Bonnet. In one hand, he holds a lantern, lit with a single candle. In the other, Phil carries a set of keys. He proceeds at a sedate pace to the archway of the Bloody Tower, where an escort is formed in readiness. This escort is made up of soldiers from the military garrison at the Tower. It comprises two sentries, a sergeant and another guard who represents the role of *drummer* with a bugle. Phil hands the lantern to the drummer, and they all march to the outer gates of the Tower. As they draw near, the Queen's guardsman steps forth. "Halt!" he bellows, thrusting his rifle and left leg forwards - the tip of his bayonet glints menacingly as it catches the lantern light, "Who comes there?"

Phil steps forwards while his entourage remains steadfast. He lifts the keys and shouts, "The Queen's keys!"

The sentry allows Phil to lock and secure the outer gates and return to the Byward Tower gates to repeat the process. As the clock strikes ten, Phil concludes the Ceremony by moving two paces forward, raising his bonnet high in the air and proclaims, "God preserve Queen Elizabeth."

The Guard answers, "Amen," as the clock chimes ten exactly. The drummer sounds *the Last Post* on his bugle. Phil then returns the keys to the Queen's House and dismisses the escort, adding, "See you in the morning, Lads!"

"Same time, same place!" replies the sergeant to moans and groans of *déjà vu* from his colleagues!

Phil rejoins Penny, Ted and Rick at Byward Tower, announcing, "I'll just change out of my Watch Coat, then we can head home!"

"That was unbelievable, Dad!" acknowledges Penny, grabbing Phil's right hand on his return. "Thank you!"

"Yes, thank you, Mr Woodville," thank Ted and Rick, standing on Phil's left.

"I'm glad you enjoyed it," replies Phil, nodding proudly. "It's a tradition going back seven hundred years and hidden from public view!"

"I loved it when the guard thrust his rifle towards you and shouted *Halt, who comes there?*" continues Rick.

"Have you ever dropped the keys?" queries Ted mischievously.

"Thankfully not," replies Phil, "it's an offence punished by imprisonment in the Tower!"

"Really?" asks Penny, concerned for her Dad.

"Only kidding!" jokes Phil, loving Penny's innocence and gullibility, adding, "No one's been imprisoned here for years."

"Not like the Princes in the Tower," replies Penny, building on their breakfast conversation.

"Exactly," agrees Phil, turning on his torch and shining it twenty metres ahead. "Let's head home along Mint Street where the Royal coins were made from thirteen hundred to eighteen ten. The Mint is one of the main reasons why the Ceremony of the Keys exists - to lock and protect everything and everyone within."

"Mum says the Mint extended around the West, North and East walls in medieval times," contributes Rick, pleased he had been listening that day! "And our houses used to be part of it."

"I heard that Isaac Newton - the fellow who discovered gravity," adds Penny, continually taken aback by the Tower's history, "used to be head of the Mint before he concentrated on physics!"

"I'm hoping to get a Saturday job at the Mint Museum gift shop," explains Ted as they walk past the entrance, "Mum says *it's got some cool stuff.*"

"You try telling that to the medieval workers who lost their fingers and eyes, forging, blanking, and stamping out silver coins by hand - exposed to deadly poisonous gases!" relays Phil, putting a dampener on Ted's enthusiasm then trying to make amends. "But I'm sure the Museum's a great place to work, Ted!"

Mint Street is cobbled and only lit by the half moon and Phil's juddery torch beam. Indistinct shapes jut from buildings and walls and trigger the imagination. Sounds reverberate left and right against the inner and outer walls, echoing everyone's voices and amplifying the smallest of sounds.

A walk in the Tower grounds at night is not for the faint-hearted. The wind whistles through the alleyways and around the Tower, drawing out historical events from deep inside the walls and giving a ghostly voice to the poor blighters, imprisoned and tortured, or worst still, executed - all stories, twisted and warped by Chinese whispers and passed down through the generations.

Phil, Penny, Ted and Rick hear footsteps behind. They freeze and turn. Phil shines his torch, but there is no one there. Phil shines his torch in all directions, high and low, but to no avail before calming the children, "It's nothing. Just the wind playing tricks."

"I'm scared!" admits Penny, gripping Phil's hand tighter and grabbing his arm, still limping from her injury.

"Me, too!" echoes Rick, moving around Ted to stand close to Phil.

"It's all in your imagination," declares Ted with cavalier disregard for Penny and Rick. "There's no such thing as ghosts!"

They approach the bend at Devereux Tower, where Mint Street turns right along the North Wall. A distant street light throws a dimly lit blanket over the cobbles to define the turning.

Phil hands the torch to Ted to lead the way so that he can take Penny and Rick's hands. He changes the subject to divert their attention. "Tell me about the infamous throw that won the competition today, Penny."

"Well, my opponent was continually attacking my weak leg," begins Penny, "and the time was ticking, and..."

She breaks mid-sentence, observing Ted stop, and start walking backwards in total silence - holding the torch out like the Queen's Guard rifle.

A sizeable bulky shadow appears around the corner, sauntering and growing with every second. No one can say anything – they are all petrified. Even Phil.

The shadow halts and then grows in stature as the *thing* or whatever it is, rises onto its hind legs, bellowing a deep and pained roar. Penny screams...followed immediately by Rick. Ted continues to walk backwards until he collides with Phil, trying to convince himself that there must be a logical explanation.

The shocking shadow turns the corner, roaring and quickening its pace. An apparition of a grizzly bear runs straight *through*, knocking the wind out of everyone, and onwards behind - one second there, the next, not - disappearing into the darkness...its roar diminishing like a tube train travelling to its next destination.

8

The Ceremony of the Liquorice!

Phil shudders and collects himself. "That was the infamous *Grizzly Ghost,*" he tells Penny, Ted and Rick, breaking into laughter to ease the tension, "I've heard all about the bawling bear but never seen it before!"

"I thought we were dead meat!" exclaims Penny, relieved to be standing and beginning to see the funny side, "It was like he sucked the life out of us - I couldn't breathe!"

"It made all the hairs on my neck stand up," relates Rick, shivering and rubbing his neck.

Ted is surprisingly silent.

"What was that about *no such things as ghosts*, Ted?" jibes Penny, poking fun at the not so cavalier convert, adding, "Feeling a little foolish, now?"

"More *ghoulish* than foolish!" retorts Ted, shaking his head in disbelief, then shining the torch under his chin to illuminate his face and mimic a ghost, wailing, "Whooooooo!"

Phil escorts them home, stopping first to drop Ted and Rick.

"What's wrong?" enquires John, opening the door and looking at each pale face in turn. "You look like you've just seen a ghost!"

"It's funny you should say that!" replies Phil, grinning and relaying the incident to John. Then they swap ghost stories like comparing war wounds, competing for the scariest ghoul in the Tower. John talks of a headless Anne Boleyn while Phil brags about Baron Hastings wandering Tower Green, using his beheaded skull to guide him! John concedes to the Grizzly Ghost, under pressure exerted by Penny, Ted and Rick, and they bid goodnight.

Penny embellishes the grizzly story for Liz before tiredness hits her right between the eyes. "I'm whacked," she declares, yawning and struggling to keep open her eyes, "What a day! Night, night!" retiring upstairs with a limp, falling into bed after token-brushing her teeth for fifteen seconds, and into a deep sleep within twenty seconds.

After what feels like five minutes. "Tap. Tap. Tap."

"Tap. Tap. Tap," repeats the distinctive sound of bird beaks on the window pane. Penny rolls onto her side to face the window, scrunching her face to begin the pained process of awakening. She opens one eye and then the other, as she closes the first! "Tap. Tap. Tap."

"Alright, guys," acknowledges Penny, stretching and yawning before throwing back her duvet and revolving her legs to sit upright on the side of her bed, shouting, "I'm coming. Keep your hair on...I mean, keep your feathers on! Talk about the early bird catching the worm!"

Penny thinks about the Ceremony of the Keys and its similarity with this repeated routine. She limps over to the window and pulls open the curtains, hollering, "Halt. Who comes there?!"

Penny opens the window and bids good morning to Gripp and Rocky, whispering, "You need to say *the Queen's Ravens*. Then I hand over the liquorice, and once you've eaten it, I finish by saying *God preserve the Queen's Ravens*. Then you *sing* the Last Post in your best voices before you fly off - concluding *the Ceremony of the Liquorice!*"

Gripp and Rocky humour Penny by cawing at the correct times and behaving for the first time she can remember!

Penny grabs her brown belt and shows Gripp and Rocky, conveying the difficulties of fighting through pain to achieve excellence. She finishes by asking Gripp and Rocky, "Have you seen the Grizzly Ghost?"

"Brarrr. Brorrr," is the reply.

"You have!" Penny plays along. "Me, too. Scary Mary!"

And with that, Gripp and Rocky depart, leaving Penny to give her ankle more attention. She sits on the side of the bed and compares ankles. The left is swollen and a darker shade of pink. Something is not right, and not because it is her left ankle!

She puts on her dressing gown and treads carefully downstairs. Liz and Phil are already halfway through breakfast, munching toast and wading through the Sunday papers.

"Morning, Penny," says Liz without lifting her gaze, engrossed in yesterday's match report, reciting, "France, England, Brazil, Belgium, Italy and Holland are through to the quarters with Scotland playing Argentina and Germany playing Greece today."

"My ankle's swollen," informs Penny, helping herself to a bowl of bran flakes and waiting for Phil to make another cup before asking for her chai latte! "It's still sore!"

"Let me look," offers Phil, gesturing for Penny to place her foot on his leg then poking and prodding, "Ooh, yes. There's something not quite right. I suggest you visit the doctor and get her opinion," he finishes, handing back Penny's foot and glancing at Liz.

"I think the surgery starts at ten on a Sunday," remarks Liz, smiling at Penny. "It'll give you a chance to shower and get ready for dragon boat training, so when your Dad clocks off at ten thirty, you'll be able to head off straight from the doctors."

"Do I have to go dragon boat training with a sore ankle," protests Penny, knowing she must be on her death bed before Liz and Phil let her miss anything. "It's just training."

"You won't be putting your ankle under any strain, so yes, Penny," says Phil, filling the kettle. "You can't let down your teammates."

"Oh, very well," accepts Penny, fluttering her eyelashes at Phil once again, "As long as you make me a chai latte!"

Phil mutters under his breath and shakes his head before smiling at his two favourite girls! After breakfast, he dons his tunic to hurry to the Byward Tower and begin the morning Ceremony of The Keys, commencing at seven minutes to nine.

One of the perks of living in the Tower is an onsite doctor and dentist. Liz and Penny sit patiently and unaccompanied in the doctor's waiting room. Penny suddenly remembers her next day dental appointment. She rubs her teeth with her tongue several times, contemplating a *metal mouth* – she is getting *train tracks!*

Dr Margaret Burgundy enters the waiting room at ten o'clock precisely. "Good morning, Liz," she says in her Belgian accent, staring down from her slender six-foot height and peering over her burgundy reading glasses, perched on the end of her nose. "'Ow can I 'elp?"

45

"It's Penny, Margie," responds Liz, helping Penny through to sit in front of the doctor's desk while Dr Margaret closes the door. "She's hurt her ankle."

Dr Margaret asks several questions and examines Penny's ankle while lying on the paper-covered burgundy vinyl bed. Penny stares around the room to note that everything is burgundy other than the magnolia walls and the white woodwork - even Dr Margaret's skirt and shoes!

"It's not broken," begins Dr Margaret, sitting back at her desk and scribbling wildly on a pad, then looking up briefly. "You'd know if it was. Ze pain would tell you!" lowering her head once more before standing to fetch something from a tall burgundy metal cabinet, continuing, "You have pulled a few ligaments which can take just as long to 'eal."

Penny smiles before realising that Dr Margaret hasn't recognised the *heel* pun!

"We can't put on a plaster cast, but we'll strap it wiz zis modern elastic device," advises Dr Margaret, approaching Penny on the bed and applying the strapping. "I will also give you some crutches to use for a few days to keep ze weight off ze ankle. So, no cycling or running or..."

"...or dragon boat racing?" suggests Penny, hoping.

Dr Margaret contemplates for a while then responds. "I zink you'll be OK wiz zat. You won't be putting your ankle under any strain," repeating Phil's words, much to Penny's annoyance.

Penny cheers up at the sight of bright yellow crutches!

9

The Old Gits, The Pretenders and The Newbies!

Dr Margaret adjusts the crutches to fit, and Penny takes to them like a fish to water, exiting the room while Liz and Dr Margaret discuss the progression of England and Belgium into the quarters.

"We are playing France," details Dr Margaret, walking out with Liz into the waiting room to catch up with Penny and check for the next patient. "It will be a difficult match. France are looking very good."

"We play Scotland or Argentina," explains Liz, watching Penny go around in circles in the waiting room. "Who knows, Margie. Belgium and England could meet in the Final!"

"Stranger zings 'ave 'appened," says Dr Margaret, waving goodbye, "but we mustn't get carried away! See you soon."

As Penny negotiates the ramp outside the Hospital Block, she finds two workmen digging a large hole. "Why are you digging a hole?" questions Penny while Liz passes the time of day.

"We're digging it ready for a new signpost," replies Fenton, the taller of the two workmen, "being put in tomorrow. Along with another two, over there and over there," he points to two different positions.

"I hope no one falls in the holes," concerns Penny, aiming her right crutch at the hole.

"Don't worry, Luv," placates Filbert, the shorter of the two workmen, pointing to a small cart, "we'll be puttin' a barrier around - 'ealth and safety and all that!"

Liz and Penny head home. Phil opens the door. He is dressed in blue shorts and an orange rugby jersey. Penny finds it funny to see her Dad in clothes other than his Yeoman regalia, but she cannot talk as she is also wearing blue shorts and an orange rugby jersey - the dragon boat club colours!

"Goodness me, Penny," remarks Phil, studying Penny's crutches, "what's the verdict?"

"Pulled ligaments," responds Penny, almost cheerily. "Dr Margaret says no cycling or running..."

"...but she did say you can do dragon boat training!" relays Liz, smiling at Penny.

"But no cycling," repeats Phil, adding, "That's put a spanner in the works!"

Penny and Phil always cycle the three-and-a-half-mile route to the Docklands Watersports Centre, just the other side of Canary Wharf in the Isle of Dogs. It takes twenty-five minutes each way. They could drive, but they do not have a car, and they have left it too late to book one of the Yeoman pool cars.

"We'll have to get a taxi," accepts Phil, looking at Penny, "but we'll need to put our skates on!"

Penny gives Phil a sarcastic look, joking, "I won't be able to get the skates over my strapping!"

"Why don't you borrow Beth and John's tandem?" suggests Liz, watching Phil and Penny crack up. "They're both working today, so they won't be needing it."

"Perhaps that's not such a daft idea!" admits Phil, convincing Penny, "It'll be fun!"

"See!" outlines Liz, "I'm not just a pretty face!"

"And a dirty neck!" jests Phil, giving Liz a peck on the cheek and heading with Penny to the bicycle shed.

Penny and Phil begin the journey. Phil pedals at the front while Penny admires the view and keeps hold of her crutches. They arrive with Phil panting and perspiring and Penny with not so much as a bead of sweat...it is hard cycling for two!

All the junior members crowd around Penny, eager to know what has happened and envious of her crutches. "Can I have a go?" asks one. "Then me," bagsies another. "Bagsy third," claims another until Penny loses count, and they must postpone when the coach calls them outside.

Phil helps to wheel three different sized dragon boats to the water's edge. They call them dragon boats, but the club commissioned a local craftsman to carve long mane lion-faced figureheads, covered in gold leaf, *roaring* with vicious-looking fangs. They mount the discarded dragon figureheads on wooden shields to hang on the club wall and record annual captaincies for the three levels - senior, intermediate and junior, affectionately referred to as *The Old Gits, The Pretenders* and *The Newbies!*

Phil is an Old Git, and Penny is a Newby! Phil's boat holds twenty paddlers, one drummer - the captain, and one steerer. The Pretenders boat holds sixteen paddlers, one drummer and one steerer. Penny's boat holds ten paddlers, one drummer and one steerer. The drummer sits at the front and provides the *heartbeat*, synchronising with the leading pair of paddlers and using a rhythmic drum beat to denote the stroke frequency.

The steerer sits at the back and steers!

Today is training, but dragon boat racing is ceremonial, and each crew honours this team-building camaraderie.

Phil is this year's Old Git captain. His crew is a mixture of men and women from all backgrounds and professions, ranging from stock market traders and lawmakers to street market traders and lawbreakers!

Penny is the *third pair right paddle*. Her crew live locally and is an equally mixed bag ranging in age from nine to fourteen. Her captain is Leroy - a fourteen-year-old *god* for whom Penny has a crush! He is the reason she comes every week, even when a cold front bears down and the wake turns to ice in the depths of winter.

Each crew performs simple warm-up exercises before returning to the start of this human-made stretch of Thames water. The coach stands on the dock, holding a stopwatch and bellowing observations before sounding a klaxon. It is not a race between each boat, but The Pretenders always give The Old Gits a run for their money, even with four fewer paddlers. The Newbies use the leading boats to raise their game, sometimes riding the slipstream to improve their time.

Penny swaps her crutches for a single paddle. Leroy bashes out a beat and brings his own sense of rhythm and rap, chanting,

"We eez
The New-beez.
Ridin' high
On waters low.
Roarin'
Soarin'.
We eez
The New-beez!"

The coach cannot complain as he jogs alongside, occasionally shouting some tactic or other. When the lactic acid burns a hole in their arms, and they are breathing three times faster than the stroke, Leroy's *Newbies* rap-anthem brings them home - the whole crew shouting *We eez The New-beez* as they cross the finish line.

"Well done, Newbies. That's a pretty good time for the first lap. Now get your breath back," instructs the coach, rearranging the crew. "Charlie, you swap positions with Mary, and Sharon, you swap with Jordan. Then we'll go again!"

The Old Gits and The Pretenders are already on the return lap, challenging each other once more. The Old Gits keep The Pretenders at bay until the end of the training session, when the advantage of youth shines through!

Penny and The Newbies do three more laps before calling it a day.

"What a workout," exclaims Leroy, beating a finale, "I know drumming isn't as exhausting as paddling, but you still get a sweat on!"

Penny stares enviously as the boys take off their tops to bask in the midday sun. The girls must suffer, or rather sweat in silence and wait till they get back to the changing rooms. Sometimes life seems so unfair!

Phil and Penny have lunch at the Dockland Watersports Centre before cycling home - everyone ribbing them as they pull away on John and Beth's tandem, singing, *"Phil-ip, Pen-ny...you'll look sweet, upon the seat, of a bicycle made for two!"*

10

We true grits!

Phil makes Penny a chai latte without even being asked! He makes a strong brew for himself, placing both cups on the table and clearing the Sunday papers into one neat pile.

Phil takes a sip, asking Penny as she peruses one of the colour supplements, "How's the chai latte?"

"You get better every time, Dad!" praises Penny, dipping a biscuit too long to see half drop in and disappear, exclaiming, "Oops!"

"How's the ankle?" continues Phil, ignoring Penny's biscuit saga, "It didn't seem to affect your dragon boat paddling."

"It did a little," admits Penny, dipping another biscuit, again too long and losing another half, "but I love paddling so much, I just ignored the pain."

"You mean, you love *Leroy* so much!" teases Phil, watching Penny turn the colour of his Watchman's Coat.

"Ohh, Daaaddd!" protests Penny, using a spoon for fishing out the biscuits only to find a slurry of chai tea crumbs. "He's the captain."

"And an excellent captain, too," approves Phil, trying to ease Penny's discomfort. "I love that thing he sings...something *New-beez...*"

Penny recites Leroy's Newbies rap-anthem, tapping the table to mimic the drummer's beat.

"I think I should have an Old Git's anthem!" suggests Phil, becoming more and more convinced, "To rally my troops."

"They're your crew, not your troops!" corrects Penny, tutting and slurping her chai latte. "You're not in the army now, Dad!"

"*We are Old Gits. Not dimwits...*" begins Phil, realising he needs help. "Please help, Penny!"

"How about, *True grits, The Old Gits?*" begins Penny, engaging her brain.

"I like it!" encourages Phil, repeating, "*True grits, The old Gits*...maybe, *We true grits, The Old Gits...?*"

"*We true grits. The Old Gits...racing fast...*" adds Penny.

"*...never last!*" contributes Phil, nodding and smiling.

"*Paddling*...what rhymes with paddling...waddling?" continues Penny, shaking her head and muttering all the words she can think of that rhyme with paddling.

"*Paddling. Battling?*" says Phil as they both nod at his wordplay.

"*We true grits. The Old Gits,*" concludes Penny.

Phil and Penny bang the table, and bellow,

"We true grits,
The Old Gits.
Racing fast,
Never last.
Paddling,
Battling.
We true grits,
The Old Gits!"
Phil and Penny *high five* and finish their drinks.

Liz works at the Crown Jewels Museum on a Sunday, leaving Phil to oversee Penny.

"How much homework do you have, Penny?" enquires Phil, loving and hating term-time Sunday afternoons - *loving* that he spends time with Penny, but *hating* that it is time spent doing homework!

"Three bits," replies Penny, surrendering to the inevitable few hours of homework. "Maths, comprehension and a model of a cell for science!"

Phil winces at the sound of *a cell for science*. He knows that the thirty-minute guide turns into at least an hour and a half and desperate rummaging for *arts and crafts* compromises!

"Let's get the maths and comprehension done and then tackle the science cell last!" suggests Phil, moving the cups and the papers to clear the table. "If we work efficiently, we'll finish in time to meet Mum and take her to the Yeoman Warders Club for supper and catch the second half of the Scotland match."

The comprehension homework is straightforward, and Penny needs little help - Phil checking for any blatant errors and spelling mistakes before she moves onto maths. Liz is good at maths. Phil is not! He is happy with addition, subtraction, multiplication and division through to percentages and fractions, but slam an equation, and not even a simultaneous one, or shove a geometry problem in front of him, and he is like a rabbit in the headlights. Luckily for Phil, Penny's maths homework is based on fractions!

Phil makes another cup of tea while Penny packs away her maths homework and reads the science sheet. "I can make either an animal or a plant cell," she informs Phil, who looks none the wiser, deciding, "I think I'll make both!"

"Both?" replies Phil, puzzled as to why Penny would double her workload, "Are you sure that's wise?"

Penny nods, beginning to imagine her creations and collecting the arts and crafts box from under the stairs. Meanwhile, Phil turns on the television to catch the pre-match ramble and mutes the sound.

Penny cuts and shapes coloured foam and sticks them to the cardboard sheet, following her pencilled underlay copied from her science textbook. She gathers cocktails sticks, applies handwritten labels and inserts them into the foam like miniature flags.

Phil continues to watch the match in mute mode. Scotland and Argentina are tentative and awkward - neither team looking to attack...or defend. Then Scotland runs the ball out of their own penalty box, passing the ball down the left side, and drawing the Argentina defence. Phil sits on the edge of his seat. England is his team, but he is one-quarter Scottish...becoming more and more Scottish as the game progresses! "C'mon, Scotland!" whispers Phil, clenching his fists and bobbing his head, "Pass the ball to the right. There are two unmarked players!"

Penny heads each cell with her best PLANT CELL and ANIMAL CELL capital letters. It is the final touch.

"Beau-ti-ful!" Phil whispers loudly as the Scotland left-winger floats the ball to the far-right side of the pitch - taken down with one simple movement. The player draws the last Argentina defender and lays the ball right. The Scotland right-winger belts it past the Argentina goalkeeper and into the back of the net.

"I've finished, Dad!" shouts Penny.

"GOOOAAALLL!" screams Phil.

55

Penny and Phil head over to the Crown Jewels. While they wait, Penny tries to see how long she can stay up on her crutches without touching the ground with her feet. Phil times her.

"I didn't expect this nice surprise," says Liz, acclimatising to the light as she exits the purposely dark museum. "Everything OK?"

"I've done all my homework!" announces Penny, proudly.

"And I didn't have to help her," informs Phil, nodding positively at Penny.

"Well done, Penny," praises Liz, removing her uniform jacket, "now we can enjoy the evening."

"We thought we could have some supper at the Yeoman Warders Club and catch the second half of the Scotland match," details Phil, taking Liz's jacket then holding her hand.

"That sounds wonderful," replies Liz, unclipping her hair. "It's just what the doctor ordered."

"Scotland was winning one-nil when we left the house," enthuses Phil, quickening the pace slightly. "So, it could be England v Scotland in the quarters!"

"How good would that be," excites Liz, happy to quicken the pace. "The *old enemies* battling each other again!"

Penny follows behind on her crutches. The novelty is still intact...just!

11

Smile like you mean it!

"Tap. Tap. Tap."

"Tap. Tap. Tap," repeat Gripp and Rocky on the window pane. Penny rolls onto her side to begin the pained process of awakening, knowing what comes next.

"Tap. Tap. Tap."

"Alright, guys," acknowledges Penny, stretching and yawning before throwing back her duvet and revolving her legs to sit upright on the side of her bed, shouting her well-rehearsed sequence, "I'm coming. Keep your hair on...I mean, keep your feathers on! Talk about the early bird catching the worm!"

Penny leaves her crutches and hops to the window. "Morning, Gripp. Morning, Rocky," greets Penny, handing each three liquorice sweets. "How are you this morning?"

Penny shows Gripp and Rocky her strapped ankle and bright yellow crutches, asking if they know Dr Margaret, hinting, "...you can't miss her. Her names Dr Margaret Burgundy and she wears...wait for it...burgundy!"

"Brarrr, Brorrr!" caw Gripp and Rocky as if to say, "Of course we do!"

"Scotland beat Argentina last night," informs Penny, hoping that the topic of football will not bore Gripp and Rocky, "So England are playing Scotland in the quarters!"

"Haw. Haw. Haw," reply Rocky and Gripp as if they know something she does not.

"I don't have to go to school till later," Penny changes the subject, giving each another piece of liquorice.

"Brarrr?" questions Gripp!

"Why? You ask," converses Penny, filling in the gaps. "Well, *brace* yourselves, Gripp and Rocky. Today's the day I get my braces!"

"Haw. Haw. Haw," reply Gripp and Rocky as if they are laughing at Penny's misfortune...or fortune if you think long term!

Penny grits her teeth, scowling at Gripp and Rocky, defending, "Take one last look at these twisted teeth, boys! From now on, you can call me *metal mouth*."

Gripp and Rocky fly off, leaving Penny to get dressed. Although she will be going to school later, still she puts on her blue and yellow school uniform. Penny brushes her hair with her special brush, supposed to make detangling more effortless and less painful. She gives up after a minute, wincing and wiping her water-filled eyes, and hops downstairs for breakfast, holding her crutches.

"Morning!" says Penny, perkily, repeating her gritted teeth scowl to Liz and Phil. "Feast your eyes on these terrible teeth. The next time you see me, I'll have a stainless-steel smile!"

"So, you'll be alright going to the dentist on your own?" asks Liz, feeling guilty but unable to shift her shift at work. "I should have organised it for after school, but I wasn't thinking. Actually...I've just remembered, the dentist only has a morning surgery!"

"I'm OK, Mum," reassures Penny, pouring the milk onto her bowl of bran flakes, "It's not as if I have to walk far, and remember, I did it once before."

"There you go, Penny," says Phil, planting a chai latte in front of Penny and smiling, "I'll be thinking of you when I rattle the keys in the gate locks!"

"Very funny, Dad!" remarks Penny, slowly shaking her head, "I'm getting braces, not metal teeth."

"I can't wait till the quarters," Liz changes the subject, adding, "it's gonna be a corker."

"I've got a bet with Hamish and Harry," admits Phil, noting Liz's disapproval, "Don't worry. It's just a fiver with each!"

"What's the bet, Dad?" enquires Penny, relishing every mouthful of bran flakes as if it were the last supper!

"England win three-two," details Phil, gulping down his tea and grabbing his tunic from behind the door.

"That's very precise," points out Liz, "surely an England win's enough!"

"John's got a bet, too," replies Phil, applying his hat, "England win two-one, so I popped for three-two!"

Phil wishes Penny good luck, kisses Liz on the cheek and disappears. Liz follows shortly, reminding Penny that the appointment is at half-past nine and that, given her ankle problem, a taxi is booked for ten-thirty to whisk her to school for morning break.

Penny sits and sips her chai latte in peace. She is feeling nervous as she contemplates her appointment. No one likes the dentist whizzing and whirling and placing strange objects orally, sucking and swirling spit-filled water - all under the spotlight like some tortured prisoner keeping schtum. If truth be told, Penny is unsettled by her dentist, although she would never tell anyone, especially her parents.

Unfortunately, her dentist, ex-Sergeant Richard York of the Gloucestershire Regiment, bears the scars of conflict. While on duty abroad, his battalion carries out door-to-door manoeuvres, looking to flush out the enemy disguising as civilians and using human shields for defence. Richard opens a booby-trapped door. It explodes, throwing him back fifteen feet in the air. The right side of his face is badly burnt, shrivelling his cheek to pull his right eye down and the right part of his mouth up. His right shoulder is smashed to smithereens leaving him slightly disfigured after surgery. His right shoulder is now higher than his left and appears somewhat hunched as he *swivels* his right arm rather than move it naturally. He grows his dark brown hair long to help hide his facial disfigurement. He is kind and thoughtful but consequently shy and nervous, avoiding direct eye contact and conscious of his appearance - especially around children like Penny. He retrains as a dentist and is one of the top orthodontists in the country. Penny wishes she could overcome her fears. Perhaps today will be different.

She sits in the waiting room, studying the adverts for *brighter than white* teeth bleaching next to various *metal mouth* pictures of the different brace types available. Very confusing.

"Penny," announces the dental assistant, lapel-labelled Anne Neville and looking directly at Penny. "Please come through."

Penny follows Anne into the whitewashed room. Richard is studying Penny's history on the computer. He glances around, looking over his raised right shoulder through his long hair and wearing a mask. "Good morning, Penny," welcomes Richard, swivelling on his chair to face Penny, gesturing, "Please climb up and let's get you comfortable."

Penny is dumbstruck. Richard is wearing a mask with the biggest printed cheesy grin she has ever seen. It is infectious. She cannot help but break into laughter, immediately relaxing and forgetting Richard's awkward appearance, stating, "I love your mask."

"I'm glad," replies Richard, smiling behind his mask and adjusting the seat and spotlight to suit Penny, "I want you to feel relaxed and that you're in safe hands."

Before Penny can reply, Richard peers over with magnifying spectacles, requesting, "Give me your best-gritted teeth scowl, please, Penny. This isn't going to hurt, but I'll occasionally be pulling. Just put your hand up if you want me to stop."

Penny nods and thinks back to this morning's conversation with Gripp and Rocky. She opens her lips and grits her teeth, closing her eyes to listen to the background radio appropriately playing *Smile like you mean it* by *The Killers!*

"What colour inserts do you want?" asks Richard, raising her seat for Penny to select from several colours. "It's totally up to you."

Penny considers the collection, initially thinking pink before deciding, "I'll have England colours, please!"

"Ah, yes, The World Cup and England are through to the quarters," nods Richard, preparing the inserts, "Great choice, Penny."

Penny bids farewell to Richard and Anne, smiling back with alternate red and white insert metal braces!

12

Roarrr!

Penny exits the Hospital block like the day before, using her crutches to propel herself down the ramp. She sees the yellow and black striped barrier surrounding the hole and looks for the other two pointed out by Fenton, the taller of the two workmen.

It has just gone ten o'clock. The Tower of London is filling with visitors, eager to beat the midday crowds and covet the Crown Jewels before the queues grow too long.

Penny wanders over to see how deep the hole is. She peers over, trying hard not to lose her balance and crash through the barriers on her crutches. By her calculation, the cavity is about two feet in diameter and nearly three feet down. It is just a *boring* hole with its excavated soil placed to the side in a conical mound, ready to be reinstated around the new signpost. Penny starts to move away. She needs to head home and grab her school bag and get down to the front gates for the taxi. Then something catches her eye sticking out of the excavated mound.

Penny looks left and right, appearing highly suspicious and acting as a lookout for a raid on the Crown Jewels. She drops her left crutch as a decoy and leans down to inspect. Then innocently and as surreptitiously as she can, she reaches across and picks out a sizeable fanglike object, a withered and worn arrow tip and a small round thin thing.

Penny puts the fanglike object in her left trouser pocket and the arrow tip in her right trouser pocket. She studies the small, round thin thing, believing it to be some coin, and places it in the palm of her left hand to scrape away most of the dirt on the *heads* side with her right index fingernail. She tries to scrape more, but the dirt is ingrained in the recesses. Penny deposits a little spit and rubs the coin with her index fingertip. She makes out the image of an angel slaying a dragon encircled and edged with Latin script. The metal begins to show a golden appearance. The Latin is hard to read, but at the bottom, beneath the image, she can make out the name EDWARD and the Roman Numeral V.

Penny stops and thinks back to Phil's description of the Wars of the Roses, muttering to herself, "Can it be? No, surely not!"

She licks the end of her thumb and begins to rub harder and harder, scrunching her eyes closed for extra effort. On the fifth rub, something magical happens.

The coin starts to grow in size, swallowing Penny's right hand then drawing in her right arm. It is like she is diving headfirst into a deep hole and turning inside out, finally pulling in her remaining arm and left hand. The coin then flips to encapsulate her like a cork entraps a model ship inside a bottle!

Penny opens her eyes and stares straight ahead. She is gazing into the face of a lion. His rancid breath makes her recoil and realise the immediate danger surrounding her. Not one but three Barbary lions encircle her. She glances left to spot the familiar outline of the Tower of London. Penny is kneeling in the middle of three lions at the Tower of London!

She glares at the coin in her left hand and rubs it again, but nothing happens. She spits on it, scrunches her eyes and tries different combinations, but still, nothing happens. Penny finds a small pocket in her long green dress and inserts the coin to revisit later.

"Roarrr!" bellows the lion facing her, rolling his head as if to call his mates to arms.

"Roarrr. Roarrr. Roarrr!" roar three lions, instilling the fear of God into Penny.

Penny places her hands together to pray, thinking this to be her last prayer before becoming supper for three hungry lions.

"What are you doing in there?" comes the question.

Penny believes it to be someone answering her prayers, but she wonders why such a question.

"I said, what are you doing in there?" again comes the question except for this time much louder - shouted by someone outside the lions' cage. "Do you have a death wish, you stupid girl?"

Penny opens her eyes and slowly turns her head to see a young boy staring at her through the cage bars.

"Please get me out," Penny asks calmly and quietly, hoping not to provoke the three lions, "I'm petrified!"

"Guard! Guard!" orders the young boy to find a willing guard awaiting his command. "Release this girl immediately."

The guard enters the lions' cage, prodding each lion with the end of his polearm weapon and thrusting his shield in defence, shouting to Penny when it is clear for her to escape. Penny runs out without a limp or any evidence of crutches. She finds it impossible to run in her green dress and longs for trousers like the young boy.

"Oh, thank you, thank you!" shouts Penny, shaking the young boy's hand, declaring, "You saved my life!"

"What were you doing in there?" enquires the young boy.

"Oh, uh..." hesitates Penny, thinking on her feet, "...I saw a fanglike object and didn't see the lions asleep in the corner!"

On the mention of fanglike objects, Penny licks her teeth to find no evidence of braces - no limp, no braces...how odd!

"You were lucky," reveals the young boy, laughing. "The lions have just been fed. Otherwise, they would tear you limb from limb beginning with a sharp bite to the back of the neck!"

Penny holds her throat and swallows deeply. "Why are there lions at the Tower?" she questions as if to divert blame.

"They are a present from some far-off ruler," explains the young boy, staring at the three lions lying in the far end of the cage.

"What are their names? asks Penny, wanting to know her previous captors.

"That one is *Primo*," the young boy points to the largest of the three lions.

"Primo?" enquires Penny, unfamiliar with this name.

"It's Latin," educates the young boy, "meaning *First.*"

Penny nods as if it all makes perfect sense.

"That one is *Secundus*," the young boy points to the smallest lion, then looks at Penny to translate, "meaning *Second.*"

Penny points to the remaining lion, anticipating, "And that one's *Third!*"

"No, that one's *Cyril!*" corrects the young boy without flinching.

"Cyril?" puzzles Penny.

"Of course not, Stupid!" the young boy disrespects Penny again as if it is perfectly acceptable, "That's *Tertius* - Third!" smiling at Penny to make up for his name-calling.

"Why First, Second and Third?" asks Penny, thinking how unimaginative.

"You mean Primo, Secundus et Tertius," responds the young boy, pointing again at the three lions, "Apparently, it's the order in which they stepped out from their journeying crate...and it's stuck ever since!"

Penny stands opposite the young boy. He is the same height and bears a similar resemblance with blue eyes, shoulder-length blond hair and freckles. His clothes are black velvet with a white ruff around his neck and long pointed shoes. He looks about twelve, but his ill-kept teeth make him look much older.

"What is your name?" asks the young boy, "And where do you come from?"

"My name is Penny," she replies, unsure what to say next but automatically responding, "my father is the new Royal Court Jester, and my mother is the new Royal Court Dance Teacher, and we live in a small house in the Tower grounds."

"I see," says the young boy with a puzzled look, "then why haven't I seen you before?"

"What's your name?" asks Penny, avoiding the question, "And where do you come from?"

"I am King Edward the Fifth," he replies simply, "and I am being kept in the Tower by my uncle until my coronation on June the twenty-fifth, two weeks from now!"

13
Hello, Sis! Hello, Bro!

Penny walks with Edward around the vast expanse of grass surrounding the White Tower and where today stands the Waterloo Block housing the Crown Jewels. Two guards follow them wherever they venture. One is taller, and they look as interested as one can be, following a twelve-year-old soon-to-be-crowned King!

"That one's Fenton," whispers Edward, pointing to the taller guard, "and the other one's Filbert."

"So, you're on first-name terms?" jokes Penny, staring at Filbert's armour, not entirely covering his protruding gut.

"I've been here since May the nineteenth," explains Edward, giving Penny one of the biggest boredom sighs she has ever heard. "Fenton and Filbert guard me from the minute I arise to the minute I fall asleep."

"Without a break?" queries Penny, wondering which party is more bored!

"There is a night guard to relieve them," expands Edward, turning with an energetic leap to face Penny, "but I never get to see them. I'm asleep!"

"Why are you locked up?" asks Penny, smiling and making a small curtsy, "You're the King."

"Let's have some fun," shouts Edward, grabbing Penny's hand. "Follow me, and I'll explain. Let's go and feed the troop."

Penny and Edward run to the northwest tower - Devereux Tower and climb the steps to the top, purveying the Tower of London and beyond. A troop of half a dozen baboons congregates around Penny and Edward and occupies the castellated parapet.

Fenton and Filbert run after Penny and Edward, knowing that Edward cannot escape, but they are following strict orders not to let him out of their sight. They arrive at the top, gasping for breath and using their polearms for support.

"Too many pies!" Edward shouts at Fenton and Filbert, giving Penny a wry smile, adding, "I did hear Cook this morning, proclaiming *Who ate all the pies?* And now we know!"

Fenton and Filbert remain silent. They are not allowed to address the King unless they are invited.

"Grab a few pieces of fruit," instructs Edward, uncovering a small wooden barrel full of on-the-turn fruit and disturbing a swarm of fruit flies, "and place them near each baboon, but don't get too close..."

"Why not?" asks Penny, picking up three squidgy apples.

"Baboons are vicious," replies Edward, lifting his sleeve to reveal two teeth marks on his forearm and pointing to a babbling baboon. "This is what that one there did to me on my first day!"

"Oooh!" exclaims Penny, taking three steps back from the baboons, "That looks painful!"

After the baboons lose interest and saunter away along the inner walls, Edward points to the central imposing White Tower - painted white to appear even more dramatic and magnificent and act as a beacon of power for all-around to see. "That is the King's palace," he states, shaking his head despondently, "from where my father, Edward the Fourth ruled and where my family lived for twenty-two years other than six months when Henry the Sixth reclaimed the throne!"

"What happened to your father?" enquires Penny, sensing Edward's sadness.

"No one really knows," replies Edward, mouthing a small prayer. "He died at the age of forty-one. I know he had failing health, but

I blame the continual stress of the Lancastrians and the Wars of the Roses. Although he didn't help himself going to war with the French a few years back - forced into a financial agreement when my Uncle Charles, the Duke of Burgundy and now deceased husband of my father's sister, Aunt Margaret, failed to assist! ...and let's not even start talking about the Scots!"

"Where were you when your father died, Edward?" asks Penny, presuming this conversation to be his first proper chat since his father's death, "It must have been terrible for you."

"I was in Ludlow with Uncle Anthony, my mother's brother - charged with overseeing my upbringing as Prince of Wales and preparing me to be King...although no one imagined that to be at the tender age of twelve!"

"Where's Uncle Anthony, now?"

"Last I heard, he's imprisoned in York," reveals Edward, dismissively, adding, "I miss him. He's my mentor and best friend, but my other uncle - Uncle Richard, my father's brother, whom my father appointed as my Lord Protector until I reach adulthood, claims that Uncle Anthony is part of a Lancastrian and Woodville conspiracy! To depose my brother and me and make some sort of a legitimate claim to the throne dating back to my great-great-great-grandfather, Edward the Third!"

"Sounds complicated!" remarks Penny, observing Edward wipe a tear from his cheek. "And unbelievably awful."

"The Woodvilles are my mother's family," despairs Edward, helplessly, "why would my own family want to do that?"

"What does your mother say about it?" asks Penny, trying to understand his options, "Surely she has some idea?"

"I haven't seen my mother to ask her," responds Edward, lowering his gaze. "Hearing about Uncle Richard's action against Uncle Anthony, she fears similar treatment, so before I arrived in London, she took my five elder sisters and my younger brother and fled from here to Westminster Abbey in search of sanctuary and has been there ever since."

"What's your Uncle Richard like?" continues Penny, eager to understand the whole picture. "Your father made him your Lord Protector, so he must be alright!"

"He unsettles me!" whispers Edward, leaning towards Penny so that Fenton and Filbert cannot hear. "He has an awkward appearance, and although he says he has my *best interests* at heart and swore an oath at York Minster on my father's death to his commitment as Lord Protector, I hardly know him. More importantly, I haven't seen any evidence of a conspiracy, and there's no way Uncle Anthony would conspire against me."

"But your Uncle Richard swore an oath to God," points out Penny. "Surely that's the ultimate commitment? Considered worse than death if not upheld."

"He says he's placing me in the Tower for my safety and to prepare me for my coronation, as have all Kings before me."

"Sounds like he does have your best interests at heart," suggests Penny, placing her hand on Edward's arm. "These Wars of the Roses have people chopping and changing their allegiances to whoever's King at the time to save their own *bacon*."

"Bacon?" puzzles Edward.

"Their land and positions of power," outlines Penny, swiping her index finger sideways in front of her neck, "and their head!"

"I wish I felt the same as you," admits Edward, "but my other uncle - Uncle Henry, The Duke of Buckingham and husband of Aunt Katherine, my mother's sister, has suddenly appeared on the scene. I think his motives are selfish, and he's overinfluencing Uncle Richard, whom, I'm sure you'll agree when you meet him,

70

is out of his depth - indecisive and better suited to the battleground than regal politics!"

"Surely Uncle Henry's wife, being a Woodville and sister of Uncle Anthony, comes under the same conspiracy theory," suggests Penny, trying to help Edward wade through this most complicated of situations.

"You'd think so," replies Edward, "but I heard from Uncle Anthony before all these shenanigans that Aunt Katherine is pregnant and is consumed with raising a small family. Also, I bet Uncle Henry doesn't tell her everything, even when he acquires more and more land from her very own family, apparently *given* to him by *my Lord* Protector, Uncle Richard!"

Penny digests everything for a few minutes, staring out across the rolling landscape on the other side of the outer walls, sporadically dotted with small holdings and tiny abodes. She concludes that the Plantagenets during the Wars of the Roses are a bunch of interrelated *wannabees*, all vying for snippets of power handed down by bloodthirsty tyrants, appearing to fight for one side but complicating this allegiance through marriage either directly or somewhere along their extensive bloodline! Although the women have no formal power, they manipulate events behind the scenes pulling heartstrings and strategically marrying for survival. It is fascinating and so medieval - almost the script for an episode of EastEnders!

"My surname's *Woodville!*" declares Penny, tentatively.

"Perhaps we're related?" suggests Edward, studying Penny and smiling, "We certainly look similar!"

"There are lots of Woodvilles," replies Penny, becoming self-conscious as Edward stares into her eyes, "and my family's definitely not part of the aristocracy!"

"You've got blue eyes like me," points out Edward. "Your hair is the same colour and length, you also have freckles, and we are identical in height."

"I know what you mean!" replies Penny, feeling her shoulder-length hair braided around the top.

"We could be confused for brother and sister!" jests Edward, extremely happy to spend time with someone similarly aged, bowing and greeting, "Hello, Sis!"

"Hello, Bro!" replies Penny, curtsying and breaking into laughter before repeating, "Hello, Bro!"

14
The Wars of the Bro-Sis!

Penny and Edward return down the Devereux Tower stairs, thinking that it is hilarious to hide in an alcove and watch Fenton and Filbert pass by and search frantically for them at the bottom.

"It's too easy!" jests Edward as he and Penny walk past Fenton and Filbert a few minutes later, "If only the guards at the front gate were like you two!"

Fenton and Filbert blame each other, knowing that their heads are at stake, then realise that Edward and Penny are nowhere to be seen. Fenton spots them and hurries Filbert to catch up.

"Have you seen the elephant or the bear?" Edward asks Penny.

"An elephant?!" cries Penny, "And a bear?!" she shakes her head in disbelief, exclaiming, "It's certainly a veritable menagerie of exotic and unusual animals!"

"Meet, Hannibal," introduces Edward, signalling Penny to wait while he approaches a tall door and opens the top section, beckoning, "Here you go, Hannibal. Come and meet Penny."

Penny feels the ground tremble as Hannibal approaches the tall door, sticking out his trunk as if to check that the coast is clear. Then Hannibal thrusts out his whole head, slobbering his long pink tongue, and revealing his enormous ears, flapping and fanning to keep cool.

"Grab some hay, Penny," Edward directs Penny to a pile behind her. "You'll soon be his best friend!"

Hannibal shakes his head in delight, trumpeting *encore* after *encore!*

"Let's wash him!" suggests Edward, convincing Penny with his enthusiasm. "He loves a good bath. Don't you, Hannibal?"

Edward orders Fenton to instruct the keeper to prepare Hannibal for a good soaking.

The keeper parades Hannibal outside his enclosure to stand calmly while Edward and Penny throw buckets of water and scrub his sides and underbelly. Hannibal is ticklish and stamps his back-right foot experiencing both agony and ecstasy simultaneously!

Edward thinks it is funny to misfire a bucket of water towards Penny, catching her full in the face.

"Right, Edward," retaliates Penny, replenishing her bucket. "It's war!"

She chases Edward around Hannibal before darting underneath and emerging to soak Edward full frontal and force him to stand like a drowned rat, not quite believing what has just happened.

"...the Wars of the *Bro-Sis!*" declares Penny, making a pun on roses and hoping that Edward can take a joke.

Edward says nothing for a few seconds before breaking into uncontrolled laughter. Penny joins in. Edward requests towels, and they dry themselves, allowing the sun to do the rest.

"Can you ride Hannibal?" enquires Penny, wondering what it is like to sit so high and look down on everyone and everything as you go.

"If General Hannibal can ride elephants through the Pyrenees and the Alps," rationalises Edward, imagining the same as Penny, "then I must be able to ride Hannibal."

"Why don't you ride Hannibal in your coronation procession?" suggests Penny, raising both arms as if to embrace Hannibal, "Just think how important and mighty you will look?"

"You're right, Penny," agrees Edward, evaluating how best to achieve. "No one will regard me as a twelve-year-old boy. Instead, they will see me as all-conquering - someone to look up to!"

Penny agrees.

"Guard," summons Edward, appearing to wake Fenton. "Fetch me some parchment paper, some ink and a quill. And, Guard," Edward instructs Filbert. "Fetch me a small desk and a stool."

Fenton and Filbert return with the requested items. Edward begins by drawing a profile of Hannibal. Penny is amazed at how good the drawing is - in proportion and bearing an exact likeness. Edward then draws a purple velvet and gold trim cover over Hannibal's back. Then he sketches a majestic oak throne with a purple velvet seat pan, high pointed back and supported side arms, finishing with elegant left and right footrests. He gives Hannibal a metal armour mask, complete with sprouting purple plumage.

"What do you think, Penny?" probes Edward while he annotates the drawing. "Is it fit for a King?"

"I think it's truly wonderful," responds Penny before realising one fundamental problem, "but how do you get on and off?"

Edward draws a grand oak staircase on wheels like airport stairs for disembarking jumbo jet passengers. "There you go, Penny."

"Perfect, Edward," replies Penny, giving the thumbs up!

"Guard," calls Edward, not fussed as to which one comes. "Take this drawing to the Royal craftsmen and tell them that they have one week to construct this so that we can train Hannibal."

Edward turns to Hannibal's keeper. "Begin familiarising Hannibal with someone riding him."

The keeper nods and returns Hannibal to his enclosure.

"Let's go and see Ursula," Edward tells Penny, leading her to another part of the Tower grounds. "Ursula, the dancing bear!"

"My mother told me about a dancing bear," says Penny, "but I thought she was pulling my leg."

"Pulling your leg?" puzzles Edward, unfamiliar with this expression. "Is this some sort of dance?"

"Not unless it makes you hysterical!" jokes Penny, confusing Edward further. "It means when someone is teasing you...telling you something that isn't true."

"Your mother is a stupid woman!" blurts Edward bluntly.

"No, she's not!" defends Penny, unhappy with Edward's disregard for her mother."

"I am...how do you say?" replies Edward with a wry smile, "Pulling your leg!"

"Ohh, you're good!" applauds Penny, smiling back sarcastically, "I have to watch you!"

Resting in the shade and curled up in a ball like a mound of raked autumn leaves, snoozes Ursula. Edward claps three times, stirring the sleeping bear to give what can only be described as a grumpy groan!

"Hello, Ursula," greets Edward, apologising, "sorry to disturb you and awaken you from your forty winks, but I have someone I'd like you to meet."

Ursula gives Penny a nonchalant nod, lowering her head to fall back to sleep. Penny shrugs her shoulders at Edward.

"Don't take it personally, Penny," reassures Edward, fetching a *shawm* trumpetlike recorder and a small drum from a wooden box nearby. "She's always gruff when she wakes up!"

Edward hands Penny the drum to beat *right hand, right hand, both hands* and repeat. He begins playing a tune on the shawm, coaxing Ursula like a Moroccan snake charmer. Ursula starts by moving one shoulder then the other, pulling herself upwards. As she stands to show her full size, Penny sees a metal chain attached to her right ankle and secured to a stake. Ursula has rhythm, stepping side to side, lifting and swaying her arms, and twisting and turning, trying hard not to entangle the chain.

Ursula roars in time to the music and gives the appearance of enjoyment. Penny is not convinced, hearing Ursula bellow a deep and pained roar as the metal anklet digs deep into her skin and reopens an old wound. Penny stops drumming and gives Edward a concerned look.

Edward stops playing, too.

15
You get pink!

"You are very talented, Edward," compliments Penny as they leave Ursula to rest with sweet honey treats and instructions to her keeper to address the ankle wound.

Edward gives Penny an assured look which might be misread as arrogance. Penny finds and picks some wild mint and puts it in her pocket, continuing, "You speak Latin, draw like an accomplished artist, and play the shawm as well as anyone," lists Penny enviously, asking rhetorically. "Is there anything you can't do?"

"When your destiny is to be King, Penny," replies Edward, walking tall, "you have to lead by example. Make decisions, engage people from a position of authority, lead your men into battle to fight your foes..."

"...or your friends!" interrupts Penny as Edward gives her a puzzled look, clarifying, "One minute taking the side of York then swapping to Lancaster and vice versa!"

"Civil War is baffling," surmises Edward, agreeing with Penny. "I don't think anyone wants it, but they're afraid of admitting it and risk losing face."

"You mean losing land and social standing, and power," expands Penny. "All perpetuated by the people in power!"

"Let's shoot some arrows!" suggests Edward, changing the subject and leading Penny to an area already set with a target and several small flags denoting distances.

Fenton and Filbert follow, then overtake to fetch and prepare two bows and several arrows.

"Have you shot arrows before, Penny?" enquires Edward, watching Penny handle her bow with trepidation.

"Not a real bow with real arrows!" replies Penny, not wanting to be outdone, "But how hard can it be?!"

"I'll go first," offers Edward, walking to the first flag. "We'll start at ten yards and see how you get on."

Edward grips the leather-bound handle with his right hand and places the arrow nock on the bowstring, licking the fletching feathers for added effect. He draws back the string with his first and second fingers, ensuring that the arrow shaft rests on his left-hand thumb, and his right cheek sits firmly against the taut string to align his right eye with the arrow shaft. Edward lifts then lowers the charged bow, calming his breath. Penny notices a slight wobble in his right arm, straining to hold the string under tension just as Edward lets go. The arrow unleashes, seeming to head three feet above the target only to drop and hit the second ring at half-past two exactly!

"Well done, Edward," congratulates Penny, stepping into position. "Stand back, everyone. This one could go horribly wrong!"

Penny tries to replicate Edward. Every time she goes to pull back the arrow, it jumps out from resting on her left thumb and dangles like a broken clock hand.

"Raise your thumb," instructs Edward, assisting Penny. "Just like that. Well done."

No sooner does Penny pull back her arrow and lay sight on the target than she lets go. Penny and Edward stare in dumbfounded amazement as the arrow appears to defy gravity, following an inverse trajectory and climbing to hit the target on the same second ring, a little later...sometime after seven o'clock!

"That was incredible, Penny," exclaims Edward as they walk to retrieve the two arrows. "I can honestly say I have never seen anything quite like it!"

"I think the feathers flew past my upstanding thumb and sent the arrow into an anti-clockwise spin," explains Penny, adding modestly. "It's just beginner's luck!"

Edward suggests that they try from the second flag at twenty yards, this time each taking three consecutive shots.

Edward sends two arrows into the second ring and one into the outer ring, frustrated that he cannot score a bullseye.

"Are you worried about becoming King?" begins Penny, keen to continue their earlier conversation.

"What do you mean, Penny?" asks Edward, collecting his arrows.

"Worried that you will be walking into the Wars of the Roses," outlines Penny, preparing her first shot, "not yet concluded and dividing your land and people within?"

"There has been little unrest since before I was born when my father and Henry the Sixth tussled for the crown," responds Edward, wondering whether Penny is overexaggerating his inherited problems, "so why should it bother me?"

"It isn't over until the fat lady sings!" replies Penny, moving on quickly before Edward can quiz her on which fat lady! "You need to figure out how you can put an end to all this inter-fighting and placate these power struggles. Unite your people to think and be as one. You've already said that there are possible conspiracies to overthrow you."

Penny hits three shots into the second ring, the third time rotating her bow horizontally to send the arrow out left to fade right.

"I'm too young to marry!" replies Edward, shaking his head at the thought, "And there are no Lancastrian suitors my age even if you count my cousins!"

Penny retrieves her arrows. Edward challenges her to a single arrow shoot-out from thirty yards, to which Penny agrees.

They retreat to the third flag. The target is small and difficult to discern. Edward prepares first.

"If it's not through war and it's not through marriage," continues Penny, "then it has to be done another way."

"Yes, but what?" replies Edward, taking aim. "That is the ten-groat question!"

Edward's arrow flies through the air, whistling a merry tune as it goes, and lands in the inner circle.

"Bullseye!" proclaims Edward, forgetting his position and performing an embarrassing victor's dance even Ursula would disown, bellowing, "Beat that, Penny!"

"You need to start by being neither *white* nor *red*," says Penny, smiling at Edward's dance then realising that he has just raised the bar.

"Are you talking about families?" enquires Edward, composing himself.

"Exactly!" replies Penny, giving Edward a side glance as she takes aim. "Families are complicated, and adults make things even more complicated."

"There's no debate there!" agrees Edward, "It's like their pride and prejudices rule their brains."

"What happens if you mix red with white?" poses Penny, unhappy with her stance and resetting her arrow.

"You get pink," articulates Edward.

"I think you should design a new rose for Edward the Fifth," proposes Penny, taking aim once more. "A pink Plantagenet rose to represent *peace and harmony.*"

"I couldn't do that," rejects Edward, shaking his head vehemently, "I am from the House of York and the white rose."

"Poppycock!" dismisses Penny, unconvinced. "You are *you*, and *you* can do or be whatever *you* want. I have a suggestion."

"And what's that?" asks Edward inquisitively.

"If I also hit the bullseye," details Penny, "then you will make your coronation pink...not red or white...or purple. Everything, and I mean everything, is pink."

Edward contemplates Penny's offer, weighing up the odds and the slim chance of a novice archer replicating his bullseye. He likes the idea of a pink rose and is happy to humour Penny - confident that her proposal will be put to bed in one missed shot!

"You're on," accepts Edward flippantly. "You're good but a bullseye at thirty yards..."

16
To marry her sister's husband's brother!

Penny releases her arrow, beginning with a horizontal bow and turning it to a vertical mid-shot. The arrow flies left, dipping towards the ground. Edward watches the arrow as if he is observing the flight of a bumblebee communicating nectar ridden directions. Penny's arrow begins to climb and pitch sideways to the right like an aeroplane taking off and heading east. Penny lowers her bow to witness the fate of the Plantagenets. Whatever happens, she has given it her best shot! Edward's mouth opens slowly at first and then stays open - gobsmacked! Penny's arrow does not land in the inner circle but bisects Edward's arrow, slicing it in half to remain lodged halfway down the shaft!

"You better close your mouth, Edward," advises Penny, shaking her head smugly, "you'll attract flies!"

Fenton and Filbert stare incredulously at each other, rubbing their eyes and discussing William Tell's apple story.

"We said *the best of three!*" says Edward, clutching at straws and following Penny to examine the results.

"Nice try, Edward," dismisses Penny, almost skipping with delight, "but I'm tickled pink!"

"What do you mean?" enquires Edward, realising the consequences.

"What I mean," clarifies Penny, looking Edward up and down and teasing, "is that you will look lovely dressed in pink!"

Penny pulls out her arrow, still intact and reusable. Edward grabs both shaft halves to dislodge his arrow. It disintegrates and deposits the arrowhead on the floor, almost in disgust. Edward picks up the arrowhead and hands it to Penny, "You must have this, Penny," he insists, staring into her eyes intensely, "it represents a turning point in history. The day that family feuds are put to one side. The day when white is mixed with red. The day the Plantagenets become pink!"

"Think of it as the day the Plantagenets are *in the pink...*" adds Penny, thanking Edward for the arrowhead and placing it in her dress pocket, "...healthy and in perfect condition!"

"You've got to show me how to shoot like that," says Edward, diverting attention away from *pink*, adding, "so that I can shoot around corners!"

"It's all in the thumb!" declares Penny, giving the thumbs up, "And there's the irony. You were the one who showed me!"

While Penny and Edward talk *pink*, another guard approaches. He bows and announces, "Your Highness. Richard, the Duke of Gloucester, invites you to his chambers for afternoon refreshments and to discuss ongoing coronation plans."

"Very good," replies Edward, reverting to King mode. "Please inform my uncle that I will bring my friend, Penny, and we will attend in thirty minutes."

The guard disappears to relay the message. Edward instructs Fenton to inform the Royal craftsmen to replace the colour purple with pink for Hannibal's throne seat. Filbert accompanies Edward and Penny to Edward's chambers inside the Garden Tower - the former Bloody Tower and stands guard while Edward changes.

"You mustn't be alarmed when you meet my uncle," Edward says to Penny as Fenton and Filbert escort them to the White Tower, "He has a spinal defect that occurred when he was a teenager and branded him with a right shoulder hunched higher than the left. And his right cheek has a serious burn inflicted in battle by the Scots a few years back which has affected his right eye and skewed his mouth marginally."

"I'm glad you told me, Edward," thanks Penny, already nervous about meeting the uncle Edward cannot trust. "It's good to be prepared."

"My Aunt and nine-year-old cousin will be there, too," informs Edward, rolling his eyes, "Aunt Anne and Edward."

"Another Edward?" says Penny, teasing, "What is it with you Plantagenets and your limited names...Richard, Edward, Henry!"

Edward laughs. "Tell me about it," he despairs, mimicking the grown-ups, "Edward, this is Edward, and Edward, this is Edward and Edward...got that Edward?!"

"What's your cousin like?" enquires Penny.

"He's fine, but he's always ill," relays Edward, unsympathetically, "and his mother doesn't allow him to do anything...other than be the apple of her eye! *Edward this, Edward that*...it's sickening! I call him *Illward*, and no one seems to notice!"

"And what's your aunt like?" Penny digs deeper.

"She has no time for me and is always dismissive," details Edward, rolling his eyes again. "I think it's because she hates my father and so consequently despises me."

"Why, so, Edward?" asks Penny, nudging Edward, "How can anyone despise you?!"

"Her father, Richard Neville, is the Earl of Warwick - Warwick the Kingmaker," continues Edward, eager to give Penny the background before they arrive. "He owned a vast amount of land and helped my father defeat Henry the Sixth and become King, hence the name *Kingmaker*. Then somehow, he and my father fall out. Warwick raises an army and restores Henry the Sixth to the throne again. My father fleas, and as a further act of defiance, Warwick gets Anne to marry Henry the Sixth's son..."

"...don't tell me," interrupts Penny, "he's called, Edward!"

"Yes, you guessed right," confirms Edward, smiling, "Edward, Prince of Wales! He is seventeen, and Anne is fifteen, and the marriage is designed to end the Wars of the Roses, merging both Lancaster and York houses when Edward becomes King and Anne becomes Queen. However, my father has something to say about this. He returns from exile to defeat Henry the Sixth and the Lancastrians and regain the crown."

"How is Anne married to your uncle?" puzzles Penny.

"As well as my father defeating and imprisoning Henry the Sixth in the Tower until his execution, Anne's father, the Earl of Warwick, is killed at the Battle of Barnet. Then her first love, Edward, is killed at the battle of Tewkesbury, leaving her vulnerable and desolate, to marry her sister's husband's brother - my father's brother and my uncle...Richard, Duke of Gloucester!"

"So, she went from being the future Queen to losing her father and her husband!" summarises Penny, intrigued by the continuing saga of the Wars of The Roses, "No wonder she despises your father!"

"And me," adds Edward, "don't forget me!"

"How does Anne treat your uncle?" questions Penny, wondering what it must be like to marry someone linked to the deaths of your father and husband and the end of your claim to the throne.

"I want to get your opinion," replies Edward as they approach Richard's chambers, "but I think she tolerates and domineers him and has ambitions on the crown for both herself and Illward...by way of seeking vengeance for both herself and the Lancastrians!"

"Enter!" comes the call as Edward knocks three times.

"Good afternoon, Uncle," greets Edward when Richard bows, "and good afternoon, Aunt," he continues, eventually seeing Anne curtsy and acknowledge him. "Where's Illward?"

"He's unwell and returns to Middleham Castle with your cousins, Margaret and Edward," replies Richard, giving Edward a look of despair and frustration at Anne's mollycoddling.

"I'm sorry to hear that," consoles Edward, turning to Penny. "Please meet my new friend, Penny."

"Pleased to make your acquaintances," Penny curtsies and introduces herself, "my name is Penny Woodville."

"A Woodville!" exclaims Richard, concerned.

"Relax, Uncle," replies Edward, smiling at Penny, "Penny is the daughter of the new Royal jester and dance teacher!"

"Not another Woodville Lancastrian commoner!" proclaims Anne rudely, "Just like your mother, Edward...using *looks* rather than status for social climbing!"

"My parents' marriage of love tried to unite our warring families," defends Edward angrily. "I demand that you apologise to Penny."

Anne mutters some form of apology, scoffing at the mention of *love*.

Penny may be a Woodville and a commoner, but she is neither a Yorkist nor a Lancastrian!

17

Love, peace and harmony!

Richard calls the maid to order refreshments. "Two goblets of wine and two small tankards of hot water with liquorice..."

"One moment, Uncle," interrupts Edward, seeing Penny's face show her dislike for liquorice. "What would you like instead, Penny?"

"Would it be too much trouble to have a side jug of warmed milk, some cinnamon and a cook's whisk!" asks Penny, awkwardly.

Anne gives Penny an impatient look but remains silent.

"Absolutely, Penny," agrees Edward, enjoying Anne's annoyance and turning to Richard, "Please order this, Uncle."

"Two goblets of wine, and two small tankards of hot water - one with liquorice and one with a jug of warmed milk, a cook's whisk, and some cinnamon spice," reorders Richard, smiling at Penny to put her at ease, "...and let's have some of Cook's plum tart!"

Edward tells Richard and Anne about finding Penny in the lion's cage and how good an archer she is...as good as any he has ever seen. Richard and Anne nod politely. The maid arrives with refreshments and freshly made plum tart.

"I don't know why you don't like liquorice," says Edward, sipping his *black liquid* after adding five spoons of sugar - a luxury afforded to the future King. "My grandfather, Richard of York, discovered some monks making it in a place called Pontefract, and the rest, as they say, is history!"

"I don't know how you can drink that black, tooth-rotting bile," dismisses Anne, sipping her red wine before declaring snobbishly. "It's the drink of peasants!"

Richard shuffles uncomfortably in his seat, diverting attention to Penny. "I am intrigued to see what you're going to do with your ingredients, Penny!"

All eyes are on Penny as she retrieves her recently picked mint from her pocket and drops it into the hot water, stirring to speed up the infusion. She places the whisk in the warmed milk, and holding the handle between her palms, she moves her hands back and forth, turning the whisk at speed and frothing the milk. She spoons out the mint and pours on the frothed milk, swirling it as she goes. To finish, she sprinkles half a teaspoon of cinnamon, raises her tankard and shouts, "Cheers!"

Edward raises his tankard and bangs Penny's, echoing, "Cheers!"

Richard joins in while Anne holds up her goblet reluctantly, half-heartedly and sarcastically whispering, "Cheers!"

"So, what do you call this drink?" asks Richard, accepting Penny's offer of a sip.

"Mint-tea chai latte!" defines Penny, delighting in everyone's surprised reactions...accept, of course, Anne's!

"It's marvellous," praises Edward, wearing a milk moustache before Penny points it out, "but it's not as good as liquorice!"

"Perhaps if you add five spoons of sugar, then it will taste better," teases Penny, "but disguise the fresh taste of mint and rot your teeth simultaneously!"

Edward gives Penny a closed smile, suddenly self-conscious of his discoloured teeth.

"Right, Edward," begins Richard, finishing his last mouthful of plum tart and summoning the maid to remove the remnants, "let's get down to the business of your coronation."

Anne purses her lips then stares out of the window to show boredom.

"You don't have to stay, Aunt Anne," suggests Edward, catching Anne off guard, "Uncle and I can discuss this."

"No, no!" responds Anne, quickly, eager to remain and influence the discussions, aggravating Edward, "I was thinking about the flowers and how fitting carnations would be..."

"The flowers have to be roses," insists Edward, sensing Anne's underlying mischievousness.

"An excellent choice, Edward," compliments Anne, manipulatively. "White roses to reflect the dominance of the House of York!" she declares, knowing this will anger the Lancastrians and build deeper divisions. "Just as we discussed, Richard."

"Actually, Uncle," Edward ignores Anne, directing everything to Richard, "I want neither white nor red roses."

"Perhaps purple then?" suggests Richard, looking for a neutral colour - Anne shaking her head in disagreement.

"I am going to be the plucky Plantagenet King that puts an end to the Wars of the Roses," continues Edward, giving Penny a quick glance, "by uniting white and red with...pink!"

"P...ink!" splutters Anne before she realises how inflammatory this will be to both sides and undermine Edward. She fakes adulation, "What a great idea, Edward. I was only saying the same thing just the other day, wasn't I, Richard?"

Anne gives Richard one of her looks. Richard nods and sighs, "Yes, Dear!"

"Everything will be pink," enthuses Edward, outlining his vision. "There will be a pink carpet laid from Whitehall to Westminster. My gown will be pink velvet lined in red and edged in white fur. Hannibal will carry me on a grand throne, upholstered in pink. The procession will have guards with pink plumes and tights, ladies in pink dresses and gentlemen in pink cravats and hats. Primo, Secundus and Tertius will lead the procession in gold cages, parading in pink coats. All my subjects, lining the streets, will be issued with pink roses and throw them down when I pass..."

Richard is speechless, trying to imagine Edward's unique concept. Anne rubs her hands together and smiles the biggest smile that Edward has ever seen her smile, thinking to herself, "Why conspire when the fool plans his own downfall?!"

Penny senses Edward's growing uncertainty, encouraging, "It will be wonderful, Edward. Fit for a king!"

"This has nothing to do with you, Young Lady," chastises Anne, much to Edward's annoyance. "This is a matter for us, not a commoner like you."

"My mind is made up, Uncle," says Edward, decisively and defending Penny. "England has to unite and lay down its arms, and find its voice through brilliance rather than bloodshed, and concentrate on the things that matter - friendship, and fighting famine and disease...not one another."

"As your Lord Protector," begins Richard, finding his voice, "My initial reaction is to imagine your father *turn in his grave*...then to bow to the stubbornness on both sides to resist such boldness. However, I will back you and assist you in this quest...but we must tread carefully and keep this a secret until the procession, where we can court your subjects and build peace and harmony from the bottom up."

"I am glad you said that, Uncle," replies Edward, reaching into his pocket for a drawing, "I want a special coronation coin."

"The design for a silver groat is underway," replies Richard, confused.

"I see that as a coin for the wealthy," surmises Edward, unfolding his drawing. "I want a coin for the people - a humble farthing. Made in gold with me portrayed as an angel slaying a dragon - the Civil War, on one side, and three lions on the reverse."

"The Plantagenet Lions," remarks Richard, perusing Edward's sketch.

"Exactly, Uncle," enthuses Edward, "But rather than a call to arms, the Three Lions represent the virtues of *love, peace and harmony!*"

"I suggest you visit the Royal Mint first thing tomorrow," suggests Richard, concluding affairs, "and I will advise the Royal craftsmen and women of your vision in pink!"

Anne finishes the rest of her plum tart, relishing every mouthful.

18
I'm a little hoarse!

"Are you up, Penny?" her mother, Liz, shouts upstairs, ringing a small hand bell as an alarm, "The sun's been up for a while now, and there's much to do!"

Penny climbs out of her bed and looks out of the window. There is no Gripp or Rocky, just people beginning their day. She opens the window to a waft of fresh human excrement, emptying into the moat and awaiting the morning tide to carry it eastwards and out to sea! Penny closes the window again. It is not a smell she can get used to, however hard she tries!

After yesterday's eventful day, Penny decides to wear blue tights with a pair of burnt orange shorts, billowing around her middle like a plump pumpkin and providing uninhibited movement unlike any corset covering dress. She buttons a white shirt and slips on a black waistcoat. Penny gives up brushing her hair when the pain of detangling outweighs the effort of achieving beauty! A simple blue ribbon holds the upper half of her hair away from her face while maintaining a shoulder-length appearance. She transfers the worn coin from her dress to her shorts pocket.

"Morning, Ma. Morning, Pa!" greets Penny as she straddles the bench and begins demolishing her daily porridge - throwing a few seasonal strawberries on top as a treat.

Her father, Philip, scribbles notes on a piece of parchment paper.

"What are you doing, Pa?" asks Penny, looking at her father dressed in his jester's uniform, except for his brightly coloured harlequin coat and fool's hat, hanging behind the door.

"Writing new material for the King's coronation!" answers Philip, rubbing his stubble and acknowledging that a shave is in order. "Here. Let me try some on you!"

"Go on, Pa," agrees Penny, always happy to be the sounding board for her father's humour. "Give it your best shot!"

"While I remember, Penny," interrupts Liz, reading from her list of things to do, "The dance troupe is meeting this afternoon to practise the coronation dances. Please make sure you are there nice and early to help me set up."

"Sure, Ma," replies Penny, reverting her gaze to Philip.

"On what sort of paper did Henry the Sixth write his last will and testament?" Philip begins his joke, standing up as if he is holding court, pretending to search the room for an answer.

"I don't know," responds Penny, repeating, *"On what sort of paper did Henry the Sixth write his last will and testament?"*

"On...beheaded paper!" delivers Philip, outstretching his arms to milk the silent applause.

"That's funny, Pa!" Penny approves, giving a thumbs up.

"Oooh, Philip," says Liz, anxiously, "I think that's a bit close to the bone! You don't want to upset the Lancastrians!"

"OK. OK!" continues Philip, "What about this one? An Earl is trying to raise an army, but there is a shortage of horses. He travels the land in search of horses without success. As he sits and ponders his problem, a pony canters over and whispers, *I hear you're looking for horses.* The Earl says, *speak up, I can't hear you*...to which the pony replies, *Sorry, I'm a little hoarse!*"

Penny and Liz laugh, repeating, "He's a little hoarse!"

"I have more, but I'm still working on them," informs Philip, pleased with the response, adding, "we get a dress rehearsal a week on Saturday. The twenty-first of June."

"How's that?" enquires Penny, understanding the coronation to be scheduled for Wednesday the twenty-fifth of June.

"There is a family reunion at the White Tower," details Liz, "when all, or most of Edward's family, arrive in London for the coronation and attend a gathering organised by Richard, the Duke of Gloucester."

Penny tells Philip and Liz all about yesterday's events, leaving out the bit about the lion's cage but detailing the baboons, Ursula, archery, and the afternoon refreshments with Duke Richard and Duchess Anne. She describes Edward's vision for a united England and his adoption of the colour pink. She swears her parents to secrecy, revealing details of the coronation farthing and this morning's visit to the Mint.

"You better beware," caution Liz and Philip, "These Plantagenets will take your head off sooner than look at it!"

"Edward's not like that," defends Penny, seeing her parents' eyebrows raise. "He's different...and he's alone, separated from his mother and siblings. He needs a friend, now more than ever."

"I'm sure that's true," warns Philip, "but from what you've said, you'd better beware of Anne and Richard, especially Anne!"

"I will," promises Penny, kissing both parents on the cheek and heading for the door, shouting, "I won't forget the dance practice, Ma, and Pa...I can't shout anymore...I'm a little hoarse!"

Penny waits for Edward outside the Garden Tower. Fenton opens the door, smiling at Penny before moving to one side for Edward to exit, followed closely by Filbert at the rear.

"Morning, Penny," greets Edward, dressed in a bottle green attire similar to yesterday's, "did you sleep well?"

"I was out for the count," responds Penny, adding," away with the fairies!"

"Are you feeling alright?" enquires Edward, concerned for Penny's state of mind.

"Pukka!" reassures Penny, embellishing, "Like a diamond!"

"You dress like a boy!" declares Edward, pointing at Penny's outfit, "The next thing is you'll be getting me to wear a dress!"

"Not today!" jokes Penny, "But you never know!"

Penny and Edward head for the Byward Tower, led by Fenton and followed by Filbert.

"Halt. Who comes there?" shouts the sentry, thrusting his polearm forwards.

"The King," replies Fenton, happy to see the sentry lower his weapon. "We are to escort him to the Mint."

The guard lets them pass and turn right onto a narrow, cobbled street, walled on both sides - Mint Street.

There is a cacophony, ringing from every building, occasionally working in harmony and resembling the insides of a clockwork timepiece.

"Please, find the Mint Master," Edward asks Fenton – who is shocked by Edward's politeness.

The Mint Master invites Edward and Penny to his office.

"I want to issue a coronation farthing," explains Edward, showing the Mint Master his doodle, "similar in design to this drawing."

"The coronation is two weeks away!" points out the Mint Master, "This is a tall order."

"But not impossible," appeals Edward persuasively.

"...not impossible," hesitates the Mint Master, examining Edward's sketch, "but this is a difficult design."

"I only need a few thousand gold farthings for the coronation launch," expands Edward.

"*Gold* farthings," exclaims the Mint Master.

"Yes. Gold farthings," confirms Edward, "I suggest you put groat production on hold and concentrate on this. I will come back in two days to sign off the design."

"Very good, Your Highness!" replies the Mint Master, impatient to inform his workers.

Penny takes out the worn coin from her pocket and studies the rear while Edward discusses details with the Mint Master. She scratches the dirt to count *one, two, three* lions...then applies a little spit. As she licks the end of her thumb and rubs harder and harder, scrunching her eyes for extra effort, something magical happens on the fifth rub.

The *supersized* farthing flips to unleash Penny's left hand and left arm, turning her outside in and ejecting her like a cannon, finally discharging her remaining right arm and right hand. In contrast, the farthing grows smaller and smaller until it is lifesize in her left palm once more.

19

Tattie tuna tombola!

Penny expects to find herself outside the dental surgery and rummaging through the excavated mound of dirt. She is not. Instead, she is walking back from school with Rick, who has kindly offered to carry her bag while she propels herself expertly down the pavement on crutches - now covered in stickers, and with pink fur added to both the handgrips and the arm supports. Penny is unsure whether to relay her recent time travels to Rick but decides not to, rationalising, "It's probably all a dream, and it won't make any sense to anyone else!"

Penny licks her teeth to find slowly breaking-in braces – she is back to the present with a limp and braces...how annoying!

"I love your stickers," compliments Rick, studying Penny's crutches. "Is that one new?"

"Yeah," replies Penny, stopping to raise her right crutch for Rick to peruse closely, "one of the boys in my class supports Germany, and he gave me the Germany flag."

"That's so cool," remarks Rick, looking at the diverse array of World Cup football team flags scattered over Penny's crutches, proclaiming, "but not as cool as the *Three Lions* sticker."

"My Mum got that for me when we bought the white England shirt," informs Penny, replacing her crutch on the ground to stable herself. "It was the last one in the shop, now that England is through to the quarters!"

Penny finds it strange to fit straight back into *today* and recall events she has missed while travelling back in time which apparently she has not! Penny shakes her head and smiles, thinking to herself, glibly, "What an imagination, Penny! Perhaps you also hit your head when you hurt your ankle!"

"Hi, Rick. Hi, Penny," shouts Ted from across the road, approaching from the direction of his secondary school.

"Hi, Ted," greet Penny and Rick, as Ted waits for several cars and a red bus to pass by before crossing the road.

"I can't wait till the weekend," excites Ted, pulling out his England scarf from his satchel and waving it high in the air with both hands, chanting, "Eng-er-land. Eng-er-land."

"It's the same night as the Yeoman Warders annual football match," points out Penny, adding, "always on the longest day!"

"The twenty-first of June," informs Rick, doing the arithmetic on his right-hand fingers.

"This Saturday," confirms Penny, showing Ted her new sticker.

"Does that mean we'll miss the match?" poses Rick, concerned.

"I hope not," responds Penny.

"I thought you knew," says Ted, trying Penny's crutches while she rests against a newly painted white wall.

"Knew what?" asks Penny inquisitively.

"Given that it's the quarter-finals, and it's England v Scotland, the Yeoman have agreed with the Royal Guard to bring their match forwards by an hour," details Ted, staring at Penny and Rick, enthusiastically. "They're putting up a large screen in the moat immediately after for everyone to watch the quarters while eating burgers and sausages."

"I thought the guards said that wasn't possible," queries Rick.

"Dad sent me a text earlier today saying that everything's been organised," Ted recites from his mobile phone after handing back the crutches, "Dad then jokes - not only do the Yeomen take on the *old guard*, but England takes on the *old enemy!*"

"It's gonna be fantastic!" excites Penny, showing Ted how it's done and quickening the pace, acknowledging, "I thought we were only gonna get to see the last quarter."

"And we get to stay up late," adds Rick, still thinking about the longest day, "it doesn't get dark until after ten!"

Penny, Ted and Rick arrive back at the Tower of London and make their way home, past the White Tower and the Crown Jewels. Penny glances around, imagining Ursula dancing with her sore paw and Hannibal stomping and shooting water as they pass. She looks up at the inner wall castellations and pictures the baboons eating their *five-a-day* after searching each other for ticks and fleas. Then Penny stops in her tracks to recall Primo, Secundus and Tertius, snarling and teeth-baring - about to treat themselves to a *ten-year-old* rump steak and fighting over left or right legs before ending on a piece of plump fresh liver! The thought sends shivers down her spine, making Penny lift her right shoulder to recall Duke Richard and his deformation.

"Are you okay, Penny?" asks Ted, seeing Penny deep in thought, "It won't be long before your ankle's better. I'm so sorry for being overzealous in Greenwich Park. I never thought..."

"...think nothing of it, Ted," interjects Penny, refocusing then fabricating, "I was just thinking about the *Grizzly Ghost!*"

"You mean…the trick of the light from the other night!" dismisses Ted, trying to appear unaffected, then diverting attention to his brother, "You still get nightmares, don't you, Rick?"

"I don't want to talk about it!" responds Rick, giving Ted an annoyed look and retorting, "You were scared, too!"

"I was definitely scared," admits Penny, giving Rick a look of support, "and we know you were scared, too, Ted!"

Ted ignores Penny and Rick, pointing at the newly installed signs. "The new signs are brilliant," he declares, leading Penny and Rick towards the modernistic sign by the hospital building. "They're more like information points with cool navigation."

Penny, Ted and Rick fiddle with the new touchscreen, inputting different commands and exploring its effectiveness before noticing the time in the top right corner of the display.

"Crikey," exclaims Penny, "it's nearly half-past five! We better get back before our parents begin to worry."

"Our parents don't worry till after six when they get back from work," informs Rick with Ted nodding his head in agreement.

"I'd better go," decides Penny, "my Mum'll be worrying."

Penny bids farewell to Ted and Rick before turning and yelling, "Hey, Ted!"

"Yep," replies Ted, looking up from the sign. "What is it, Penny?"

"Do you know anything about the Princes in the Tower?" quizzes Penny, raising her eyebrows.

"Not much," replies Ted, racking his brains, "only that their uncle killed them to become King Richard the Third. Why?"

"Oh, no reason," responds Penny, not wanting to raise suspicion and fabricating, "we're learning about them in school and given that we live here, I thought I should find out more!"

"I'll ask my Mum," offers Ted, helpfully, "she's an expert on all things medieval!"

"That's OK, Ted," cries Penny, heading home and testing her ankle with more pressure, concluding, "I'll ask my Dad."

Liz and Penny sit and chew the fat before making dinner. Penny abandons her crutches and hobbles around the kitchen, helping to toss the salad and lay the table. At the same time, Liz boils a few potatoes and three eggs, opens a tin of tuna and a tin of anchovies, and pulls it all together to create her infamous salad niçoise, nicknamed *tattie tuna tombola!*

Phil walks in at six-fifteen. He removes his tunic and hangs it behind the kitchen door, venturing over to kiss Liz on the cheek before turning to Penny and greeting, "Hi, stranger!"

Penny looks at him in shocked surprise.

"I haven't seen you for a couple of days!" continues Phil, sitting.

"Uh...uh," hesitates Penny, unsure how to respond and unwilling to tell her parents about the magic farthing and her travels back to medieval times.

"What with me having to leave early two mornings on the trot and then staying out to watch the France Belgium game last night!" finishes Phil, smiling fondly at Penny.

Penny draws a deep breath. Phew...False alarm!

20
Swaying Trees!

"Tap. Tap. Tap."

"Tap. Tap. Tap," repeat Gripp and Rocky on the window pane. Penny sits up with a start, excited at knowing what comes next.

"Tap. Tap. Tap."

"Alright, guys," acknowledges Penny, throwing back her duvet and clambering out of bed, eager to see Gripp and Rocky and happy to shout, "I'm coming. Keep your hair on...I mean, keep your feathers on! Talk about the early bird catching the worm!"

Penny hurries over to the window. Her ankle feels much better but is not one hundred per cent. "Morning, Gripp. Morning, Rocky," greets Penny, handing each three liquorice sweets and deep breathing the fresh dawn air. "How are you this morning?"

"Brarrr. Brorrr. Brarrr!" caw Gripp and Rocky as if to say, "Where've you been?!"

"You're never gonna believe it, guys," enthuses Penny, delighted to be telling her story, albeit to two sweet-beaked birds feigning interest. At least they will not, or cannot reveal her secret!

"Caw?" squawks Gripp, tapping the windowsill to request more liquorice.

"I've met Edward the Fifth and Richard, the Duke of Gloucester...and his wife, Anne Neville," begins Penny, generously depositing three more bits of liquorice each and talking ten to the dozen. "Although, Anne is a bit of a bossy woman, and Edward doesn't trust her!"

"Haw. Haw!" reply Gripp and Rocky as if they know Anne and are expressing their agreement.

"Edward's being held in the Garden Tower - now the Bloody Tower, until his coronation," continues Penny, alternating her gaze between Gripp and Rocky, "unable to leave…a prisoner, although Duke Richard says it's for his protection! Edward's mum and siblings have taken refuge in Westminster Abbey, and he hasn't seen them…even after the death of his father. It's so sad. And Duke Richard is claiming that Edward's mother's Lancastrian family is conspiring to undermine Richard's role as Edward's Lord Protector and take charge of Edward, which has led to Duke Richard imprisoning some of Edward's close family like his Uncle Anthony. It's all such a mess!"

"Brarrr. Brorrr," caw Gripp and Rocky, beginning to lose interest.

"And I met three lions named Primo, Secundus and Tertius," continues Penny, hoping that talk of animals will reinvigorate their interest, "and babbling baboons…and an elephant named Hannibal…and Ursula, the dancing bear!"

"Haw?!" squawks Rocky, becoming extra-fidgety.

"Ursula, the dancing bear!" repeats Penny, "And Edward's going to end the Wars of the Roses with a pink coronation…and issue a gold farthing…just like the one I found. Stay there. I'll show you."

Penny risks Gripp and Rocky flying away to find her medieval farthing. She searches her school uniform and finds the withered coin stuck deep at the bottom of the right trouser pocket. The lion's tooth and Edward's arrow tip have somehow found themselves onto her bookshelf, alongside her collection of homemade slime and overpriced collection cards!

"See!" Penny shows Gripp and Rocky both sides - the tarnished gold shimmering subtly in the morning sun. "The rear has three lions just like Primo, Secundus and Tertius, and the front has Edward the Fifth shown as an angel slaying the dragon of Civil War."

"Tap. Tap. Tap," Gripp and Rocky push their luck and demand more liquorice!

Penny ignores them, continuing, "It's a magic farthing. I don't know how but when you rub the front, it takes you back in time, and when you rub the rear, it returns you back to the present. Watch!"

No sooner does Penny scrunch her eyes closed and complete the fifth rub on the front side than she disappears *inside out* into the consuming coin and travels back in a haze of swirling darkness - wrapped in a floating mix of red, white and pink petals.

"Penny. Penny," shouts her mother, Liz. "Are you with us?"

"Oh...uh, yes, Ma!" replies Penny, frantically looking around for clues as to her whereabouts. "Sorry, I was just thinking about something!"

"Concentrate, please," orders Liz, now Penny's dance teacher. "And that goes for everyone!"

Penny smiles at her co-dancers, all dressed in black velvet practice dresses and rehearsing the coronation dances. Penny loves dancing but not quite as much as her mother, who loves choreographing spectacular performances to suit every royal occasion.

There are twelve females in the dance troupe and range in age from ten to eighteen. Penny has two other girls - Mary and Margot, who are the same age and similar in height. There are three girls aged twelve, another three aged fifteen and the remaining three, aged sixteen, seventeen and eighteen.

"Right, Girls," rallies Liz, grabbing their attention by clapping three times, "Let's go over the *Swaying Trees* routine!"

Penny and the girls assemble in four rows of three, ordering by age and height – the youngest at the front. Liz gives the nod to the musicians – a mandolin, a flute and a drum player. Row by row, the girls lift their arms above their heads and begin swaying their hips and arms in a clockwise rotation. As the music tempo increases, they start revolving their arms independently to their swaying hips as if the wind is blowing stronger and stronger. Then they converge towards the centre, still swaying, and then move back outwards, repeating to pulse like a brewing storm.

"That's good, girls," encourages Liz, also swaying in time with the girls and correcting, "Penny, Mary, Margot. You need to move your heads more."

"This feels stupid!" remarks Penny, much to her mother's annoyance. "What have *Swaying Trees* got to do with Edward's coronation?"

The music peters off, and all the girls unite in mutiny!

"What do you suggest?" poses Liz, perturbed by the mass disapproval before defending her idea, "I thought *Swaying Trees* represent the turbulent times we live in, and then we're going to end with collective calm and ensuing peace!"

"How about portraying Edward as an angel...who searches the woods for the tyrannical dragon, representing the Civil War," suggests Penny with all the girls nodding.

"Go on, Penny," insists Liz, pleased that it is Penny with the bright idea, "I like it!"

"The three elder girls can be *the head*, *the body* and *the tail* of the dragon, covered in red and white scales like rose petals depicting both sides," details Penny.

"And the dragon blows fire!" contributes Mary.

"Exactly!" agrees Penny, smiling as the three elder girls begin to imitate an angry dragon. "Then eight girls, dressed in pink satin to represent a forest of unified harmony, encircle the dragon and sway just as before, initially concealing the dragon until they move outwards..." continues Penny, positioning eight girls around the dragon before finishing her description. "Then the last girl...who could be me, represents Edward - dressed in a halo, shiny metal armour, and holding a sword...weaves in and out of the trees in search of the dragon..."

"...then the trees pull right out to allow Edward to confront the dragon," enthuses Liz, brandishing Penny with a makeshift sword and instructing the musicians to create an accompanying tune. "And ends with Edward thrusting his sword into the dragon's belly and standing victorious!"

"We can call it *King Edward, the Dragon Slaying Angel!*" proposes Margot.

"I love it!" excites Liz, shuffling the girls into position. "It's a sensational showstopper!"

21

Treason of the highest order!

"Good morning, Duke," says Penny, curtsying even though she is wearing her orange pumpkin pants and blue tights again. "It's a fine day today, Sir!"

"That it is, child!" replies Duke Richard, exiting Edward's Garden Tower chambers and enquiring, "Are you coming to see Edward?"

"I am, Sir," responds Penny, seeing the concern in Richard's face, "Is he available?"

"He is suffering from a toothache and runs a small fever," answers Richard, pulling out a linen cloth from his pocket. "This is not the first time. It seems to be a running problem...perhaps a sign of other underlying ailments."

"Or too much sugar!" jokes Penny, apologising when Richard shows no reaction.

"The doctor has instructed a poultice of red rose water, softened beeswax, and butter to be applied with a linen cloth like this one," informs Richard, shaking his head, "but Edward refuses to apply. Perhaps you can persuade him?"

"I think I know what will change his mind," replies Penny, taking the linen cloth. "Leave it with me!"

"I am enjoying the mint-tea chai latte!" divulges Richard, smiling and rubbing his stomach, "Very tasty! Anne is loving it, too but insists on no milk...or cinnamon!"

"Just *mint-tea*, and not the *chai latte* bit!" replies Penny.

"I suppose so," agrees Richard, heading back to the White Tower and jesting, "whatever makes her happy!"

Penny looks for pink roses but settles for white roses, growing up the side of the Garden Tower. She knocks on the White Tower kitchen door and asks Cook for a few cloves which Cook gives her with puzzled looks and moans about the cost!

Penny passes the time of day with Fenton and Filbert as they open the door to Edward's chambers and finds Edward forlorn and staring out of the window. "I hear from your uncle that you're feeling unwell, Edward," starts Penny, pulling up a seat beside him.

"The pain is unbearable," exclaims Edward, holding his jaw with eyes closed, "I want someone to extract the tooth with pliers immediately, but I don't want a toothless grin for my coronation!"

"I have brought some white roses to add to the poultice!" reveals Penny, placing the bunch on the table. "I thought you would like to fuse white with red to create a pink concoction!"

"I like your thinking," replies Edward, breaking off several petals and adding them to the mortal before grinding them with the pestle. "The thought of Lancastrians taking credit for my remedy fills me with utter distaste!"

"Once you've applied the poultice," continues Penny, reaching for the cloves in her pocket, "I suggest you place a clove on the affected tooth to help numb the pain while we venture outside to take your mind off things!"

"Uncle Richard informs me that a select few of the Council members are meeting today at the White Tower to clarify procedures for his role as Lord Protector and agree on final arrangements for my coronation," converses Edward, cringing at the poultice smell. "I want to attend, but Uncle Richard says that this is contrary to his representation. It fills me with concern."

"You have to trust him, Edward," encourages Penny, "otherwise it'll drive you mad...and besides, you're in no fit state to attend with an excruciating toothache!"

"I'm feeling a little better, Penny," admits Edward, forcing a smile. "Thank you. Let's go and throw some hammers!"

Penny ties a temporary linen cloth around Edward's jaw with a double bow on the top of his head. It is to help retain the poultice and alleviate the pain. Edward catches sight of himself on a reflective surface and immediately removes it, running both his hands through his long golden locks. Fenton and Filbert escort Penny and Edward outside to Tower Green.

"Hello, Edward," bellows the voice of an imposing figure crossing the Green towards the White Tower. "How are you, Your Highness?"

"I find myself with a bout of toothache, Baron Hastings," replies Edward, happy to see a familiar face and introducing Penny, adding, "but other than being cooped up here and unable to see my mother and siblings, I am fine, thank you! And you?"

"I am well, considering the circumstances," answers William Hastings, a close ally and loyal servant to Edward's father - lowering his voice as he draws near. "I am glad to say that your mother and siblings are well and reciprocate their sadness and longing to see you."

"Have you seen them?" enquires Edward, murmuring and repeating, "Have you seen them?"

"I took my son-in-law, Thomas - your stepbrother, with a good friend of ours, Jane Shore, to visit them a few days ago," whispers William before changing the subject and jeering, "hammer one home for me!"

Edward hands Penny a hammer as William disappears inside the White Tower, describing how Duchess Anne is William's niece,

110

the daughter of William's wife's sister, adding yet more complication for Penny to follow!

Penny can see that Edward is distracted and distant, apparently reflecting on and missing his family. He then regains composure, challenging Penny, "Furthest throw chooses lunch dessert!"

Lord Stanley, Bishop Morton and Bishop Rotherham walk past bowing ceremoniously at Edward and head for the Council chambers.

"Having fun, Edward?" shouts a portly figure, red-faced and out of breath.

"Running late for the Council, Uncle?" questions Edward, about to throw first.

"That I am!" replies Uncle Henry, the Duke of Buckingham, scuttling past towards the White Tower, "And I need to talk to Duchess Anne before I attend...no rest for the wicked!"

Edward shares his mistrust of Uncle Henry with Penny. Edward feels impotent and exposed to unsavoury characters, eager to reignite Lancastrian claims, but he must trust his father's appointment of Uncle Richard to uphold his best interests.

"Right, Penny," restarts Edward, trying to smile through his clove-clenched mouth, "where were we?!"

Edward swings his hammer between his legs and propels it forwards on the third swing. The spherical weight drags its trailing handle like a comet through the night sky and lands with a thud about forty feet away. "Beat that, Penny!" he cries.

Penny begins by mimicking Edward and swinging the hammer between her legs. Then she adopts a different method, rotating her body and swinging the hammer in a circular motion by pivoting on her left foot. She releases the hammer on the third rotation, planting her right foot firmly in front. The ball shoots like a cannon shot, passing Edward's attempt and landing with a dull thump some ten feet further down the field. Edward is speechless once more, and so is Penny!

As Penny and Edward fetch their hammers, they hear the Council in session, debating and discussing, sometimes with raised voices – it is another hot summer's day, and all the windows are open. They can also hear Henry talking to Anne in an adjoining room.

"Psst!" beckons Edward, holding his index finger to his lips for silence, then whispering, "Follow me, Penny."

Penny and Edward walk casually as if they are going to the side of the White Tower. As soon as Edward deems that they are hidden from view, he darts sideways, lowering his back and scurrying like one of the babbling baboons. Penny follows closely behind in the same fashion. Penny and Edward stop under Anne's window and stretch cautiously to hear the conversation.

"So, what you're saying, Henry," clarifies Anne, pacing up and down, often gazing out of the window and almost discovering Penny and Edward. "Is my Uncle William visited Elizabeth Woodville at the Abbey with my brother-in-law, Thomas Grey ...your nephew and Edward's stepbrother, along with Jane Shore – a woman determined to get her claws into the Yorkist family!"

"That's right, Anne," confirms Henry, adding fuel to the fire. "As you know, my wife...Katherine, although with child and tending to our young family, is in regular communication with her sister in the Abbey..." pauses Henry to ensure utmost secrecy. "...And she informs me that there is talk of treason to overthrow Richard as Lord Protector and place young Edward directly on the throne to influence power for Lancastrian gains."

"Are you sure, Henry?" questions Anne, "These are grave accusations, and one might conclude that it is you who will benefit from the Woodville demise, despite your marriage to Katherine, because of your affiliation and loyalty to Richard."

"I would tell Richard myself," offers Henry, "but he still feels uncomfortable with the imprisonment of Earl Rivers, Anthony Woodville - Edward's uncle and mentor. And he listens to you, not me, who, as you say, will appear to gain from such a claim."

"Very well, Henry," resolves Anne, "I cannot risk Richard being overthrown and for me to be discarded alongside. Especially given that should anything happen to Edward or his brother, then Richard will become King, and I will become Queen, and my son, Edward, will become heir! Inform Richard that I need to speak with him."

Edward looks at Penny with a look of complete bewilderment, but they must remain silent and clandestine. Henry disappears for Richard to appear two minutes later.

"Henry says you have called for me, Anne," says Richard, impatiently, "can you not see that I am engaged in important matters on behalf of King Edward, and I am establishing myself as Lord Protector?"

"I do not care about the boy King, Richard," dismisses Anne, "It is you and self-preservation that concerns me most!"

Edward and Penny listen as Anne tells of treason and an immediate threat to Richard's life, instructing, "Get rid of him, Richard. Show me you are strong and worthy of marriage!"

Richard returns to the Council. Edward and Penny shuffle along the wall to stand under the neighbouring window.

"You seem agitated, Richard," observes William. "Is everything alright with my niece, Anne?"

Richard cannot sit nor look anyone in the eye, occasionally glancing at Henry in disregard for placing him in this position.

Henry sits silently...smirking.

Richard knows that if he does not act, he will be disobeying his deceased brother and endangering the safety of Edward while also putting his own life at risk. Richard fidgets with the hilt of his sword, empowering and motivating as if he is going into battle, finally exploding. "As Lord High Constable of England and Lord Protector of King Edward the Fifth, I accuse you, Baron Hastings," turning and pointing at William, "of treason...of the highest order!"

"Don't be absurd, Richard!" denies William, looking to the other Council members for support, "I am a loyal servant of Edward the Fourth."

"But not Edward the Fifth, Baron! The evidence is clear...that you, together with your son-in-law, Thomas Grey and Elizabeth Jane Shore are conspiring with the Woodvilles to exercise treason against our monarch," condemns Richard, standing tall and disguising any stoop or spinal disfigurement, commanding. "Seize him, guards, and take him immediately to Tower Green and remove his head from his body for all to see!"

The guards rush William. He is consumed with anger and denial, which rapidly turns to transparent fear as the guards march him outside to an area hidden from Edward and Penny. Two guards hold each arm and force him face down on the executioner's block. Another guard applies a black hooded mask, grabs hold of the menacing axe still varnished in previously spilt blood and raises it to William's screams of, *"God will be my defender!"* and drops it with one fell swoop.

Edward and Penny hear the thud of the axe wedged into wood followed closely by a lesser thud like that of a coconut falling in a fairground sky.

Then there is a moment of ghostly silence.

Primo, Secundus and Tertius go berserk, smelling *fresh kill.* The baboons scatter in a heightened frenzy of deafening noise.

Ursula lets out a pained roar. Hannibal trumpets a sad lament. Richard looks at Henry and turns away in contempt. Anne releases a sigh of relief. Edward and Penny sit, sobbing - the tears rolling down their cheeks, unable to console themselves...Edward's toothache turning into heartache.

22
A secret so great!

Penny and Edward sit frozen to the spot, aware of the commotion above and on the other side of the White Tower. The Council members shout their objections at Richard. Bishop Morton and Bishop Rotherham storm out of the meeting and leave as quickly as possible through the Byward Tower. Lord Stanley remains to argue with Henry. Anne has conveniently disappeared.

Richard orders two guards, "Do not place Baron Hastings' head on a spike outside the Tower for public display," Richard reasons, feeling the adrenaline rush change to one of guilt. "Place his body in a box with his head held between his hands facing heaven and store him in St John's Chapel until I issue further instructions."

"What worries me, Penny," whispers Edward, wiping his tears, "is that Richard acted on Anne's instructions albeit in my honour and for my protection."

"But Anne is...acting on information...relayed to her...by Henry," sobs Penny, almost unable to string words together, "without...confirmation...or hesitation!"

"William was condemned to death without a fair trial," points out Edward dismissively. "Executed as an act of murder!"

"The sooner you're crowned, the better," remarks Penny, her sobs now turning to sniffles.

"I wish it were that simple!" replies Edward, shaking his head and acknowledging, "Too many people would rather I quietly disappeared. Aunt Anne. My mother's side of the family. And then there's Uncle Henry with his distant claim to the throne!"

"Richard wants to keep you as King," contributes Penny, trying to help. "Anne may want you out of the way, but she has to protect Richard. Otherwise, she's gone too. Your mother's family

- let's call them the Lancastrians, need you and your brother to become King. Otherwise, Richard will be King, and as for Henry, he's a fly in the ointment. He's pulling strings behind the scenes which could see you and your brother...and Richard...all disposed of, providing him with a legitimate claim to the throne as a Lancastrian descendent!"

"I started with toothache," responds Edward, rubbing his jaw and swallowing hard, "which moved to heartache," Edward massages his head before dropping his head into both hands and declaring, "and now I've got the biggest headache ever!"

"And who wouldn't?!" sympathises Penny, consoling Edward by rubbing his back. "What's important is to trust Richard, who, I'm sure will honour and protect you...and who will ultimately manage Anne, but you must get Richard to distance himself from Henry - he's the snake in the grass!"

"You're right, Penny," concedes Edward, breathing in deeply. "I need to discuss things with Uncle Richard and persuade him to retrieve my younger brother so that he can protect us both!"

"Good thinking, that man!" encourages Penny, seeing the burden of power on Edward become lighter for a few seconds.

"There's something in the back of my mind that's worrying me," admits Edward, delighted to talk things through with Penny.

"What's that?" asks Penny.

"The cousins that Uncle Richard mentioned the other day," begins Edward.

"Margaret and ooh, what's his name...Edward?!" jests Penny, further lightening the mood.

"Yes, Margaret and...Edward!" smiles Edward, "They are Aunt Anne's sister's and Uncle George's children...my father's younger brother before Uncle Richard, whom my father executed for treason."

"Your father executed his own brother!" exclaims Penny, "How can things get any more ludicrous?!"

"Some say he was drowned in a butt of wine," details Edward, beginning to smile before realising his insensitivity, "for trying to overthrow my father and take the throne for himself."

"What is it with *men* and *power!*" comments Penny.

"Don't ever be fooled," retorts Edward. "Women may not have a direct claim to the throne, but they all have the same hunger for status and power. Mark my words!"

"That, I don't deny!" replies Penny, understanding more and more about the period. "What were you saying about George...?"

"My father didn't need to execute him, but there are rumours that George harbours a secret about my father and some bishop," relays Edward, leaning over to Penny and whispering, "a secret so great it threatens to undermine all that my father stands for!"

"What's the secret?" questions Penny, on the edge of her seat.

"That's just it," answers Edward, "it's a secret that died with my Uncle George and my father. I wish I knew."

"The plot thickens," jokes Penny, gesturing for Edward to stand. "What's important is to stay strong and carry on as normal...or as normal as being imprisoned in the Tower of London can be!"

"Thank you, Penny," says Edward, brushing himself down, "I can't tell you how indebted I am to have you by my side."

Edward and Penny retrieve their hammers and begin their mini-contest once more, deciding to let the dust settle and the blood dry before confronting Richard!

Aunt Anne appears with Lord Stanley and Uncle Henry, escorting them to the main gates.

"Good meeting, Uncle Henry?" shouts Edward, causing the three of them to stop and look around.

"You are going to have a wonderful coronation, Edward," responds Henry, nervously glancing at Anne and Lord Stanley.

"Did you *execute* everything you needed to?" probes Edward mischievously, enjoying watching Lord Stanley shift from one foot to another and Henry turn a ruddier shade of red.

"I think your pink vision is inspired, Your Highness," compliments Lord Stanley. "The fresh vision of youth!"

"I was just talking about next weekend, Edward," interjects Anne, changing the subject, "and extending the invitation to Lord Stanley and his wonderful wife, my long-standing friend and Henry's aunt, Margaret Beaufort!"

"Very good, Aunt Anne," agrees Edward, nodding his approval, "The more, the merrier when a family reunion is involved!"

"Katherine and I will be there, too," informs Henry, smiling at Anne, "Although we may leave early because of our young children and Katherine now being with child once more!"

"Of course, you will be there, Uncle!" replies Edward, "You *are* family after all!"

23

Air shoes!

"Hi, Pa," murmurs Penny, returning home after agreeing to meet Edward the following day and revisit the Mint before meeting with Richard. "Where's Ma?"

"She's at the costumiers, Penny," replies Philip, adjusting a pair of wooden poles, "helping to make the pink dresses and that fantastic dragon costume you and she dreamt up. Apparently, the armour makers and the carpenters are involved in lending their metal and woodworking skills. Your mother says they're making something even that Italian fellow would be proud...what's his name...the one who's making all the noise in the art world currently...Leonardo somebody..."

"...Da Vinci," aids Penny, slightly downbeat.

"Why the long face, Penny?" enquires Philip, unused to her doom and gloom.

"Did you see or hear the execution today?" asks Penny, trying hard not to become emotional again.

"I didn't, thankfully," replies Philip, leaving his poles to give Penny full attention, "but there's word going around that it's Baron Hastings."

"It is, or rather, it was Baron Hastings," confirms Penny, shaking her head, "executed by Duke Richard without a trial or a jury."

"I don't think you should be troubling yourself with such things," responds Philip. "I'm sure Duke Richard had a good reason."

Penny enlightens Philip on the earlier events and Edward's predicament. Philip warns Penny to distance herself from Edward and how like today, it could all end in tears. Penny defends her position and convinces Philip that she will be careful. She compromises by offering to distance herself if Edward's younger brother, Richard, arrives.

"What are you making, Pa?" questions Penny, feeling more upbeat.

"You know how I've been working on my jokes," begins Philip, retelling the *little hoarse* punchline. "Well, I was thinking how it might be funny if I had some props."

"How do you mean?" queries Penny, looking at the ten-foot poles and jesting, "To keep the audience back when you tell a bad joke!"

"Ha. Ha. Very funny!" replies Philip, lifting up one of the poles. "I asked the jousting organisers if they had any old lances, and they gave me these two."

"And...?" encourages Penny, eager to hear the explanation.

"I've taken two-foot off the sharp end," demonstrates Philip, enthusiastically, "and used the off cuts to create a perpendicular handle one-foot down from the top. Then foot pegs fixed a further three-foot down and pointing inwards to make foot platforms, some six-foot above the ground."

"I still don't get it, Pa," puzzles Penny, rubbing one of the handles.

"I also asked the blacksmith for two horseshoes," adds Philip, showing Penny two u-shaped iron shoes and smiling a third *u-shaped* smile. "Hold the pole, Penny, and I'll nail each one to the top of each pole," instructs Philip, placing three nails in his mouth and hammering in a fourth nail, "to create arm supports, like so!"

"But I still don't get it, Pa!" further puzzles Penny, turning her head sideways to view each horizontal pole.

"All will become clear!" continues Philip, hammering the last nail into the second horseshoe, warning, "Stand back, Penny!"

Philip takes both lances, inserting his arms into the horseshoe supports and gripping each handle. He elevates the lances off the ground and starts running. After ten strides, Philip plants both ends of the lances onto the ground and launches himself into the air. Just before he's vertical, he places each foot on the protruding pegs, screaming, "Look, Penny. I'm walking in the air!"

Unfortunately, the lances have inserted into grooves in the ground. Philip can't lift either lance and falls flat on his face, yelling, "Crikey, Penny. I'm falling from the air!"

Penny helps up her father. They're both in fits of giggles while Philip checks for broken bones!

"I think they're great, Pa!" praises Penny, "You crazy man!"

"Perhaps if you hold them while I climb on from the downstairs window," suggests Philip, dragging his lances home, "then I can start from a standing position."

"Sounds like a good plan, Pa," remarks Penny, still sniggering at the memory of her father's faceplant. "Where did you get the idea?"

"I had to go to Westminster Hall yesterday to check out the coronation venue," explains Philip. "The cart I was in broke a wheel, so I offered to walk the remaining way to save time and be picked up after the wheel repair. Anyway, there was this alley, and I'm not exaggerating. It was knee-deep in human waste, running down to the river. The smell alone would anaesthetise any pig!"

"That sounds revolting!" comments Penny, wafting her hand over her nose. "What did you do?"

"I had two choices. Either walk back and try another route," draws out Philip as if he is telling a joke. "Or wade right through! But I look at my new shoes and think there must be another way. Finally, I see this long pole leaning against a wall. I take the pole, or rather, I borrow the pole," corrects Philip, giving Penny an educating look, "take a run-up and stab the pole into the knee-high muck...catapulting me across. On the other side, I start thinking about how I could use two sticks to walk across then how great it would be to create *air walking* shoes!"

Philip disappears inside to open the downstairs window. He employs a stool to help him clamber onto the windowsill, gesturing for Penny to come closer and place each lance against the wall. Philip positions each foot and then each arm, awaiting the right moment.

"Right, Penny," says Philip, checking the coast is clear and for any hiding holes, "after three. One. Two. Three."

Philip moves the right lance first, followed quickly by the left lance, followed quickly by the right lance until he is walking, albeit like a toddler taking his first steps, wobbling and about to fall at any moment. "I'm walking, Penny!" howls Philip, seeing if he can stop and balance on the spot, "The view's fantastic from up here!"

"I want to try," pleads Penny, staring up at her father enviously, "and be like Hannibal!"

"These poles are too big, but I can make you a smaller set when we get the other side of the coronation," responds Philip, walking backwards and then forwards, almost showing off!

"What are you gonna call them, Pa?"

"Air shoes!" replies Philip, joking, "Shoes to look down on people without being snobbish!"

"You should paint them yellow and wrap a pink ribbon around," suggests Penny.

"Good idea, Penny," agrees Philip, "Good idea!"

Liz arrives home clutching several pink dresses and ensuring they do not drag along the floor.

"Hello, wife!" hollers Philip as he walks above Liz, now shrinking cowardly between his two poles. "How's life down there?!"

Penny stands and laughs, seeing her mother bemused and scared simultaneously.

"What are you doing, Philip?" shouts Liz, disapprovingly, "You nearly made me drop all these new dresses!"

"Air shoes!" replies Philip, turning around.

"Air, what?" questions Liz, beginning to see the funny side.

"Air shoes!" shout Penny and Philip together.

"My new shoes for the coronation!" adds Philip, "I'm going to paint them yellow and wrap pink ribbon...and tell jokes from up high!"

"Whatever next!" surrenders Liz, turning to Penny and joking, "Penny. Take my advice and do not grow up to be like your father!"

"I think Pa's air shoes are great!" defends Penny, giving Philip the thumbs up. "Once people see them, everyone will want a pair. It'll be the next craze!"

"Beats shoes with bells on!" yells Philip before imagining how bells could be a clever addition.

"Yeah, yeah!" replies Liz, beckoning Philip and Penny, "Let's have dinner, and Penny...I need you to try this pink dress on for size."

24

Still no eye-deer!

"Tap. Tap. Tap."

"Tap. Tap. Tap," repeat Fenton and Filbert on the door. Philip orders Penny to answer the door while he finishes his breakfast. Liz has already departed for the costumiers, complaining of too much work and not enough hours in the day.

"Tap. Tap. Tap."

"Alright, I'm coming," shouts Penny, unlatching and slowly opening the front door, "keep your hair on!"

"Good morning, Penny," bows Fenton as Filbert steps back and checks his hair, puzzled by Penny's welcoming comment.

"Good morning, Fenton," replies Penny, looking over to acknowledge Filbert. "Good morning, Filbert."

"King Edward wonders whether you are ready to join him?" enquires Fenton, acting as a messenger, continuing cordially, "He and Hannibal request the pleasure of your company."

"Who is it?" Philip shouts from within.

"It's the King, Pa!" replies Penny, trying not to fluster her father.

Penny hears Philip knock over his chair and run around, frantically clearing dishes and putting on his tunic before appearing behind.

"Hello, Your Highness," greets Philip, bowing and buttoning his tunic.

"This isn't the King!" corrects Penny, embarrassed by Philip's mistaken identity. "This is Fenton, and this is Filbert. Edward's personal guards!"

"Where's the King?" questions Philip, looking beyond Penny and glancing left and right.

"He's with Hannibal," informs Fenton, pointing in the direction of Hannibal's enclosure.

Then Edward and Hannibal appear across the Tower Green. Edward is sitting on his throne, attached to Hannibal's back just like his sketch. Moments later, he orders Hannibal to stop, or at least Hannibal's keeper, walking alongside and leading with a long stick. Hannibal trumpets their arrival.

"Hi, Penny," yells Edward from up high. "Isn't this marvellous?"

"It's beyond marvellous," declares Penny, leading Philip out to meet Edward and Hannibal, "It's unbelievellous...super fantasicable!"

"The carpenters have even put in a small compartment to store food and refreshments should I get hungry or thirsty along the way," details Edward, demonstrating by throwing Penny an apple.

"This is my father, Edward," introduces Penny, pushing Philip forwards.

"Hello, Mr Woodville," shouts Edward, dipping his head respectfully.

"It is a pleasure to meet you, Your Highness," replies Philip, bowing so profoundly he nearly falls forwards!

"Penny tells me you are the new jester," converses Edward, smiling at Penny and then Philip, "and your wife is the new dance teacher."

"That is correct, Your Highness!" responds Philip, detailing, "We are here to entertain you. I tell jokes, and my wife arranges the most spectacular dance renditions."

"I believe you will be performing ahead of my coronation at my family reunion this weekend," continues Edward, immediately taking Philip by surprise by demanding. "Tell me a joke!"

"Right now?" asks Philip, unexpecting Edward's request, seeing Edward nod enthusiastically. "Certainly, Your Highness!"

"Why don't you do it with your air shoes!" suggests Penny, noting the discrepancies in height.

"That's a great idea," whispers Philip, disappearing back inside.

"Air shoes, Penny?" questions Edward.

"Wait and see, Edward," replies Penny, tittering, "They're amazing!"

The downstairs window bursts open and out poke Philip's air shoes, closely followed by Philip, clambering onto the windowsill and mounting the bright yellow poles, he stayed up late to paint. Philip *air walks* over to Edward and looks him in the eye! Edward is dumbstruck and looks at Penny as if to say, "What's going on?!"

"What do you call a deer with no eyes?" begins Philip, walking back and forth so as not to fall.

"I don't know!" responds Edward, repeating, "What do you call a deer with one eye?"

"A good eye-deer!" delivers Philip, immediately following with, "What do you call a deer with no eyes?"

"I don't know!" responds Edward, repeating, "What do you call a deer with no eyes?"

"No eye-deer!" continues Philip, immediately following with, "What do you call a dead deer with no eyes?"

"I don't know!" responds Edward, repeating, "What do you call a dead deer with no eyes?"

"Still no eye-deer!" finishes Philip, clumsily lifting his hands to welcome applause.

"Excellent, Mr Woodville," praises Edward, clapping approval and nodding favourably at Penny. "I look forward to the weekend!"

Philip jumps down from his air shoes and bids Edward farewell, leaving Penny to follow Edward back to Hannibal's enclosure, where he dismounts using the new staircase on wheels. Fenton and Filbert escort Penny and Edward to the Mint and the expectant Mint Master.

"Welcome, Your Highness," bows the Mint Master, turning to face Penny. "Good morning, Penny."

"I can't wait for a moment more!" excites Edward, rubbing his hands in anticipation.

The Mint Master presents Edward with his gold farthing, informing, "We thought it best to strike a sample for your approval, Your Highness, rather than delay with endless drawings."

Edward examines both sides. He says nothing, exploring all the details and the correct inscriptions. Penny watches the Mint Master nervously fidget behind his back and break into a sweat!

"This is superb, Mint Master," proclaims Edward to smiles and sighs of relief. "It is exactly as I envisaged. Thank you."

"You are most welcome, Your Highness," responds the Mint Master, positively signing to his assistant, who exits to instruct full steam ahead. "We serve to please!"

Edward shows Penny the farthing. She sees why he is delighted – it is an exact replica of her withered coin, buried deep inside her pocket for safe keeping and the subsequent *return journey.* Edward hands back the *one-fourth penny* to the Mint Master, who immediately bows and responds, "That is for you to keep, Your Highness!"

Penny and Edward return to the Garden Tower. Edward has arranged for Richard and Anne to join them for lunch on the presumption of discussing the coronation!

"I think the gold farthing is the best coin I've ever seen," compliments Penny, as they pass the sentry who is hollering, *"Halt. Who comes near?"*

128

"Thank you, Penny," replies Edward, adding immodestly, "It is rather good...even if I say so myself!"

"I've seen the coronation dances, and I assure you," continues Penny, "you won't be disappointed!"

"I look forward to the weekend when I get to see a select few," replies Edward, stopping to reflect.

"What is it, Edward?" questions Penny, second-guessing, "Is it the meeting with Richard and Anne?"

"A little!" replies Edward, expanding, "I wanted a meeting with Richard alone, but Anne insisted on being present! No, it was another thought I was having...!"

"Do you want to tell me?" probes Penny, not wanting to presume.

"It's about your father," discloses Edward.

"Oh, I'm sorry, Edward," apologises Penny, probing, "is it his jokes? My mother and I keep telling him that they're inappropriate!"

"No, it's not that!" dismisses Edward, chuckling.

"Then what?" puzzles Penny, concerned.

"I want him to lead the coronation procession on his air shoes!" requests Edward, smiling.

"Oh, Edward!" shouts Penny, playfully pushing, "I thought it was something sinister!"

25
Top-that!

"Welcome, Uncle. Welcome, Aunt," greets Edward, ushering Richard and Anne to a table laden with lunch, "I'm so glad you agreed to dine with me in the Garden Tower. We have so much to discuss."

"Why is this girl here?" Anne points at Penny disapprovingly and without glancing. "These matters do not concern her."

"Penny is my guest," defends Edward, chivalrously pulling out a seat for Penny, "and as King, I expect you to do respect that."

Anne whispers under her breath, "Not for much longer..."

"What was that, Aunt?" questions Edward, holding his right hand to his ear, "I didn't catch that."

"Nothing, Edward," replies Anne, curtly then diverting attention. "Let's eat. I'm starving."

There is an array of cold meats, a cheese selection, various vegetables, bread and an assortment of condiments. Richard, Anne and Edward are bemused as Penny takes the carving knife and cuts two slices of bread, places slithers of ham and cheese on top of one of the slices before adding a little onion and spreading mustard on the other slice and topping her concoction. She cuts her *layered lunch* in two and holds one half to her mouth. On seeing everyone staring, Penny goes, "What's wrong? Have you never seen this before?"

"Never!" declares Edward as Richard cuts similar slices for him and Anne before handing Edward the knife. "What do you call it?"

"A *Top-that!*" blurts Penny, inventing another name for the humble sandwich, catchphrasing, "Your choice of toppings held captive between two slices!"

"I've seen *open* variants across the Channel," contributes Richard, "but never *closed* like this!"

"It's a ridiculous name," dismisses Anne but enjoying her first mouthful.

"I don't know," says Edward, joking, "it's difficult to *top that!*"

They spend the next five minutes discussing combinations and how they should introduce the *Top-that* at the family reunion. Richard and Anne wash it down with a goblet of wine while Edward and Penny savour the sweet taste of freshly squeezed apple juice.

"I want to talk to you about my brother, Uncle," starts Edward, stirring sugar into his apple juice.

"What about your brother?" responds Richard, sipping his wine.

"I am concerned for his wellbeing," replies Edward, grimacing as the sugar attacks his sore tooth.

"He is held in the sanctuary of Westminster Abbey," details Richard, "and he is perfectly safe albeit in hiding."

"I am not so sure..." continues Edward, tentatively, unsure how to broach the subject of William's execution, diplomatically phrasing, "I have heard of further conspiracies."

"These are being dealt with," reassures Richard, purposely ignoring Anne's stare, adding. "As your Lord Protector, I am taking all necessary precautions to ensure your safety and seat on the throne. I have six thousand soldiers coming from the north to quash any Woodville rebellion. To send a strong message to the Lancastrians that I mean business and that Edward the Fifth will become King on the twenty-fifth of June...resuming sole power when you reach adulthood."

"That is reassuring to hear, Uncle," responds Edward, pouring Penny and him another glass of apple juice, "but I still have concerns for my brother. Surely it is better for you to protect us both, regardless of any longing I have for my mother and siblings?"

"Edward's right!" declares Anne, much to Edward's surprise, "What happens should anything befall Edward?"

Richard says nothing, listening intensely and staring at the ceiling for inspiration, knowing how indecisive he can be.

"Edward continues to have a toothache after a toothache," describes Anne, almost too enthusiastically. "What if Edward follows in the distressing footsteps of his sisters, Mary and Margaret, dying young, or his brother, George, succumbing to the plague?"

"You make a valid point, Anne," admits Richard, nodding and examining Edward. "My oath to God and all my efforts to fulfil my brother's wishes would be in vain."

"Then there are the rumours being circulated by one of your Council members, Richard," continues Anne, mischievously, curling a wry smile at Edward. "Bishop Stillington."

Penny looks at Edward. His face turns white as he recalls his father's secret, probing, "What rumours, Anne?" turning to Richard, "Do you know anything about these rumours, Uncle?"

Richard fidgets and shifts uncomfortably on his chair. "They're just rumours, Edward!" dismisses Richard, giving Anne daggers, "Unconfirmed tittle-tattle."

"You must tell me, Uncle," insists Edward, "especially if they involve my brother and me."

Richard hesitates before finally divulging, "Bishop Stillington claims that your father was betrothed to another before your mother."

"Lady Eleanor Talbot!" reveals Anne, enjoying every minute as Edward sits squirming and looking to Penny for consolation.

"So, what!" shirks Edward, "My father married my mother."

"If these rumours are true, and that's only an *if*," continues Richard, delicately, "and this prior marriage was not annulled before your mother's marriage, then this makes you and your siblings illegitimate," pauses Richard before delivering the final blow. "Meaning you and your brother will have no claim to the throne!"

Anne disguises her smile by pretending to rub her nose. She can almost detect the sweet smell of succession!

"Are you sure that these are just rumours, Uncle?" concerns Edward, seeking concrete reassurance.

"Absolutely, Edward," replies Richard, nervously...knowing that the rumours might have some credence.

"Then let's get my brother, Uncle," orders Edward. "Immediately."

"Yes, Richard," pushes Anne, excited that events are naturally falling into place, "bring the two Princes together...under one roof."

"Let's wait until my army from the north arrives," suggests Richard, reluctant to enter a place of holy sanctuary.

"No, Richard," disagrees Anne forcefully. "Act immediately!"

"Why not send Uncle Henry?" proposes Edward, uneasy and unused to colluding with Anne, "Let him be seen to do this."

Penny knows that this will also test Uncle Henry, giving him an opportunity to deliver Edward's brother to the Lancastrians!

"Guards!" shouts Richard, "Send for the Duke of Buckingham!"

Anne feels that her job is done and excuses herself from Edward's chambers. Edward takes this chance to quiz Richard.

"Why do you allow Aunt Anne to manipulate you, Uncle?" questions Edward directly. "She seems to control you?"

"It's complicated!" confides Richard, candidly. "Firstly, I feel at home on the battlefield brandishing a sword. Otherwise, I find myself indecisive...at least I think I am...I can't decide!" jests

Richard trying to lighten the mood, continuing, "Anne gives me direction. Secondly, I feel indebted to her after sacrificing much of her inherited land to my brother, George and her sister, Isobel, to secure her hand in marriage. And thirdly...and perhaps most importantly, she blames me for having only one child - Edward and his constant ailments, as if my disfigurements have, in some way, affected him from birth."

Edward consoles Richard, finishing on brighter things by showing Richard the new gold farthing. Richard departs to instruct Uncle Henry, promising to deliver Edward's brother by sundown.

Penny and Edward pass the time by playing chess and chequers, followed by endless card games.

As Penny gets up to return home, the door opens, and in walks Fenton, followed closely by a rather timid and frightened young boy.

"Rich!" screams Edward, running to his brother and embracing.

"Ed!" screams Richard, scrutinising Edward. "Is it really you?"

After brief introductions, Penny makes a quiet exit, leaving them deep in conversation and reminiscing. Remembering her promise to Philip, Penny finds her coin, scrunches her eyes, spits and rubs *Three Lions* five times.

Sure enough, magic happens once more!

26
Five turnips to four!

"Good day at school, Penny?" enquires Phil, grabbing the paper and turning to the back pages to catch up on the World Cup news.

"Fine!" replies Penny with the enthusiasm of a damp squib.

"Just fine?" mocks Phil, needing more feedback. "Not fantastic?!"

"Just fine, Dad!" repeats Penny, walking back from the microwave with reheated tea to sit at the table, slurping.

"I see you're walking much better," observes Phil, lowering his paper momentarily. "Perhaps you'll be fit enough to join in the youngster's kick around at this weekend's get together?"

"I should be," replies Penny, rotating her ankle. "I couldn't do this a few days ago!"

Penny looks forward to the annual summer solstice get together. This year lands on a Saturday, which means no school the next day and a late night! There are three more days to go. Penny cannot understand why time plays tricks. The more she wants time to speed by, the slower it seems to go as if time is trying to annoy her deliberately! Saturday finally arrives.

Penny hurries her morning meeting with Gripp and Rocky to race downstairs only to find a note reading. *Dad is busy with John all day, preparing the moat. I'm working this morning. Then I'm meeting Beth to fetch groceries for a mammoth salad making session! Make your way over in good time...you don't want to miss Dad leading the opening ceremony! Then it's the quarters. C'mon England! Here's a tenner for lunch. Love Mum x*

Penny hangs around with Ted and Rick all day. They wear their England shirts - Penny and Rick in white and Ted in red because England is playing Scotland uncharacteristically in red. They revisit Greenwich Park and share a foot-long French baguette stuffed with ham and cheese, a little onion and spiced with mustard, prepared in a local delicatessen by an ultra-friendly attendant named Anne!

They return to the Tower of London and jostle like babbling baboons for prime positions along the outer wall, looking down on the narrow football pitch marked with red and white lines in the dry moat below. There are two makeshift goals at either end, resembling gigantic lobster pots with nets strung inside oak frames. To call the impending game *football* is a misnomer. It is its predecessor - *Gameball*, although over time it is much closer. Now, they use a football rather than an inflated pig's bladder, but there is no offside rule...in fact, there are no rules whatsoever!

Penny can see Liz and Beth, with several others buzzing around like busy bees at the north end of the moat. They are arranging the open buffet alongside the barbecue, which is beginning to smoke as one of the Yeoman ignites it using a dry squib, breathing life into leftover charcoal from last year's event!

Just before kick-off, a guard, dressed in full regalia, sounds the bugle and the accompanying drummer beats a *call to arms!*

Phil appears from around the north end outer wall, holding a red and white pentagon-spotted ball and leading his team of *warriors*, dressed in a white kit which includes knee-length shorts and long-sleeved laced shirts. They stand in front of their goal and spread full width. Penny counts thirteen Yeoman players.

Thirteen guards appear at the south end, marching in single file beneath the main entrance bridge. They are dressed in an identical styled red kit and brandishing polearms, dispersing across the entire width and advancing to the drummers slow beat towards the halfway line.

Then like an All Blacks haka, the guards thrust their polearms towards the Yeoman and yell, "Halt. Who comes near?"

Phil marches forwards, spearheading his team now arranged in a triangular formation. At ten paces, Phil outstretches the football and shouts at the top of his voice, "The Queen's football!" placing the football on the centre spot while the guards withdraw arms and retreat to their goal, securing their polearms in a large wooden box. Penny, Ted and Rick cheer for the Yeomen, competing with the Royal Guard contingent.

The guard blows his bugle to begin the game. Pandemonium ensues as twenty-six unsupervised grown men create mob rule, following no apparent laws and using both sides of the moat wall to assist. Somehow the ball finds its way into one goal or another occasionally. There is no scoreboard. Instead, the drummer beats his drum and puts a turnip on a spike. After thirty minutes of mayhem, it is three *turnips* to two, to the Royal Guards!

There is no half time or changing ends, just one hour of frantic football, played at an ever-decreasing pace as tiredness sets in and age surrenders to youth!

In the dying minutes, Phil retrieves the football and pretends to roll out before spying John lingering on the right side, hidden in shadow and pulling away from his nearest opponent to create space. Phil wellies the ball upfield. John collects the ball as it ricochets off the wall, dribbling past one player intent on slide tackling, then past another before belting it into the back of the *lobster pot* as the bugle calls full-time! The Yeomen win five turnips to four! It is like a battlefield with twenty-six bodies strewn around the moat, all gasping for breath before the Yeomen gather around the centre and cry *three cheers.*

The goalposts are carried to the south end while Penny and the crowd arrive to help distribute chairs in front of the large screen, wheeled from around the corner like some medieval catapult.

Everyone queues for food before finding a seat to watch the game. They collect a paper plate and shuffle down the line, precariously piling more and more onto their plates like a house of cards, susceptible to the slightest movement.

A lone piper marches in from the south end. The Scotland supporters roar while the England supporters stare at each other, mocking then enviously wishing for a similar tradition. The national anthems are sung, but the sound of the lone piper is dramatically stirring, albeit short-lived, as the distinctive warble starts to grate and resemble an animal in distress!

All the children follow suit, wearing *roaring* facemasks. Penny, Ted, Rick and the other England supporters have roaring tigers while the Scotland supporters wear long hair Highland cattle, complete with horns, lowing the loudest *mooooo* imaginable!

Ted sends his small drone upwards to record the birds-eye view for posterity. Rick holds Ted's phone to view the transmitted image. Penny, Ted and Rick cannot believe their eyes. As a complete stroke of luck, the odds of which are a *brainache* to calculate, now that everyone is seated and munching burgers or crunching salad, the audience of perfectly distributed red and white England shirts and blue Scotland shirts is an exact representation of the Union Jack flag!

Scotland gives England a good *hiding* in the first half, putting two past the keeper and almost adding a third after a disallowed penalty. The second half serves to rekindle the cliché of *a game of two halves* as England resurfaces as a different team, running Scotland in circles and drawing equal within fifteen minutes. Scotland tries to recompose, but there is something magical about England as every move finds them deep in the Scotland half, rampaging to the final whistle and a five, two victory.

Penny hears the lone piper lay down his deflating bagpipes - groaning disappointment.

England celebrates reaching the Semi-finals. Cheers sound nationwide...*Three Lions on a shirt* singing from the top of every building and echoing around the moat.

"Coming for the kick about, Penny?" ask Ted and Rick, removing their masks.

"Yeah, in a minute," replies Penny, eager to find out how Edward and his brother are coping, "I need to spend a penny!"

Penny looks fondly at her worn-down *Three Lions*, turning them over to apply some spit and rub the gold farthing five times while she scrunches her eyes closed.

𝕿𝖍𝖊 𝖒𝖆𝖌𝖎𝖈 𝖍𝖆𝖕𝖕𝖊𝖓𝖘 𝖔𝖓𝖈𝖊 𝖒𝖔𝖗𝖊!

27
Weddings, funerals and coronations!

"Are you ready, Penny?" Liz shouts up the stairs, tapping her foot impatiently and muttering to herself, "She'd be late for her own funeral!"

"Three minutes, Ma," Penny shouts back, applying some makeup for theatrical effect. "Have you got my breastplate?"

"It's down here," replies Liz, staring at the brightly polished breastplate armour and wooden sword, painted to look like the real thing which is too heavy for Penny.

"Are you nervous?" Philip asks Liz, wearing his new harlequin suit as per Edward's instructions - red and white diamond check quarters juxtaposed with pink satin quarters and a similar hat complete with chiming bells. "This is our first Royal performance ahead of the coronation."

"Don't remind me, Philip," retorts Liz, helping Philip with his hat, "I could do with a few more weeks practice. Our dragon looks about as fierce as an eager puppy!"

"Hopefully, Edward's relatives will be more focused on reacquainting than passing judgement on our performances," suggests Philip, tying Liz's dress at the back, adding, "but I'm good and ready for any hecklers!"

"I know you have court privileges, Philip," concerns Liz, applying more white makeup to Philip's face and neck, carefully avoiding the black crosses over his eyes, "but today's hecklers might be tomorrow's King!"

"It's not the Kings I'm worried about!" jests Philip, checking his bag of tricks and collecting his air shoes, "We know who wears the trousers!"

"And don't you forget that!" jibes Liz, turning to welcome Penny. "Finally. Any longer, and I'd have to stand in for you!"

Liz compliments Penny on her makeup and pink satin floor-length dress. Penny places her *Edward* costume in her bag together with the breastplate, halo and sword.

"If only I had my oils," jokes Philip, admiring Penny and Liz's vision in pink, "and I'd paint a picture for posterity!"

Penny saw Edward and Richard playing outside earlier in the day. Both are nervous at seeing all their relatives for the first time, many of whom are travelling from afar and arriving in advance of Edward's coronation, even before reaching their London residences.

Penny, Philip and Liz head for the White Tower to join the other performers. Penny peeks inside the Grand Hall and marvels at the long banquet table, laid with gold platters and silver goblets alongside a cascading buffet of the finest food she has ever seen, topped with a posing peacock displaying its feathers and gilt covered feet.

"Hello, Penny," greets Edward, appearing from behind a curtain and pinching a few chicken drumsticks from the buffet table and handing them to Richard, still hiding behind the curtain, "We're hungry. The relatives were supposed to be here an hour ago, and we got bored waiting. Want one?"

"Do you think that's a good idea?" worries Penny, warming to the thought.

"Hey, I'm King," dismisses Edward, handing two more drumsticks to Richard, "Who's going to dare stop me?"

"So why are you hiding behind the curtain?" queries Penny, holding back the curtain to view Richard laden with drumsticks and chomping a mouthful, unable to talk. "Hello, Richard!"

"It's all part of the fun," defends Edward, handing Penny a drumstick then changing the subject. "I like your pink dress."

"Thank you, Edward," says Penny, holding a grease-ridden chicken leg, "I can't get my dress ruined, especially before the performance."

"Call me, Ed and Richard, Rich, Penny," replies Ed, handing her a napkin. "Wipe your hands and face on this when you're finished."

"I can't believe the King of England and the Prince of Wales are stealing food!" teases Penny, "Commoners are imprisoned for lesser crimes!"

"It's not stealing," justifies Rich in between mouthfuls, "just eating ahead of time!"

"Why don't you come outside and meet our relatives when they arrive?" proposes Ed, "There will be lots of children."

"All named Edward and Richard, I presume!" replies Penny, "I'd love to, but I have to get ready."

"Nonsense!" dismisses Ed, gesturing towards the door, "The performances don't start until everyone is seated and onto the second or third course."

"Oh, very well," accepts Penny, following Edward and Richard outside, kidding, "if you insist, Your Highness!"

"I do!" persists Edward, "You are at my beck and call, *Lowly Subject!*"

Penny, Ed and Rich sit on Tower Green, watching the baboons run along the inner wall castellations and occasionally stop to mimic a series of face pulling gargoyles!

Fenton and Filbert stand *at ease* close by. Richard and Anne wander outside, smartly dressed and relishing the late afternoon sun.

"It's a shame Edward is still unwell," remarks Rich, addressing Anne, "I would like to have met him, given we are the same age."

"I am hoping the sun will aid his speedy recovery," answers Anne, giving her husband one of her dismissive looks. "Thank you for your concern, young Richard."

A guard enters the Tower Green, escorting the first arrivals.

"Hello, Sister," welcomes Richard, approaching and kissing Elizabeth of York, the Duchess of Suffolk on both cheeks, "I trust your journey from Suffolk was plain sailing and uneventful?"

"Hello, Brother. It was uneventful but monotonous!" responds Elizabeth, turning to Ed and Rich, "Hello, boys!" curtsying, "Your Highnesses!"

"Hello, Aunt Beth," reply Ed and Rich, "So lovely to see you. And Uncle John...it's a pleasure!"

"The pleasure is all mine, Your Highnesses!" replies John De La Pole, the Duke of Suffolk, bowing then turning to Richard and Anne, "Richard. Anne. I was only saying to Beth on the way down how we only get together at weddings, funerals and coronations!"

"How true!" smirks Richard, glancing behind John, "And these must be my nephews and nieces. Oh, how they have grown!"

"Yes, Brother," interjects Beth, poking, "If you weren't away fighting all the time, then you would have seen them more often!" introducing her children, "John is twenty-one, Elizabeth is fifteen, Edmund is twelve, and Humphrey is nine!"

"We left the other four children - Anne, Catherine, William and Richard at home," adds John, indicating their diminutive height. "We thought it best not to bring such young children to the coronation...running around and getting lost and all that!"

A slender six-foot woman, dressed in black and unescorted, breezes into the Tower Green, broadcasting with a slight French Belgian accent, "Brother! Sister!"

"Margie! Are you all alone?" enquires Richard, approaching Margaret, the Duchess of Burgundy and kissing both cheeks several times in a continental way, "We weren't sure whether you would make it today or tomorrow!"

"The Channel was like a mill pond," replies Margie, smiling and radiating her innate beauty, "and we sailed down the Thames with equal ease and cast anchor just outside," waving towards the river then scolding Richard. "Of course, I am alone, Richard. You know my husband, Charles, died in battle, and I have no children, and now I am mourning my stepdaughter's death...Mary."

"How insensitive, Richard," reprimands Anne, shaking her head at Richard before consoling, "I am so sorry, Margie."

"Richard! Anne!" shouts Henry, bounding into the Tower Green carrying two four-year-olds, Elizabeth and Henry, and followed by his pregnant wife, Katherine, holding the hand of five-year-old Edward, "What a lovely evening for a banquet!"

"It would be even better if you hadn't imprisoned my brother, Anthony...Richard York!" Katherine directs her anger at Richard before turning to smile at Edward and curtsy, "Your uncle and mentor, Your Highness!"

There is an awkward silence. Penny sees Edward despair at his conflicted allegiances and the ever-diminishing numbers at these family reunions!

28
Knock, knock!

"Perhaps Katherine, your brother, Anthony," states Richard, ignoring Anne's stares, "should not have plotted against my dead brother's wishes to appoint me as Lord Protector for the safe succession of his eldest son, Edward...through to adulthood."

"Since when has delivering a son to his mother been a crime?" questions Katherine, also giving Henry daggers, "Answer me that, Richard."

"When the *mother* is aligned with the scheming Lancastrians, looking to benefit from the close alliance of a young and impressionable King," replies Richard, involving Henry and accusing. "This is rich coming from you two! You and Henry are doing very nicely out of the Woodville demise - forcing your own sister into hiding, Katherine..."

"...let's not spoil the evening, Katherine," interrupts Henry, caught in the middle and uneasy with the attention, appealing to both Katherine and Richard, "this is a time for celebration and unity."

"Exactly!" exclaims Margie, "I haven't travelled all this way for another family feud. Leave your indifferences at the door. Thirty years of infighting only breeds discontent and bitterness!"

The appearance of another guard, escorting Lord Stanley and Margaret Beaufort, helps diffuse the tension...momentarily!

"What are they doing here?" quizzes Beth, looking puzzled at John before turning to Richard, "They're not family, Brother!"

"I invited them," admits Anne, stepping forward to welcome Thomas and Margaret, then pointing to Henry, "Margaret is Henry's Aunt...so, she is family...albeit through association!"

"It wouldn't surprise me if Baron Hastings and Katherine Neville are also invited," responds Beth. "Your Uncle and Aunt, Anne!"

"That's enough, Sister," orders Richard, reluctant to reveal William's execution, "Anne and Margaret have been friends for years, and Edward gave his consent, didn't you, Edward?"

"Are we all here?" asks Edward, bypassing comment, rubbing his stomach and jesting, "I could eat a little horse!"

"A little hoarse!" jokes Penny, realising that no one has heard Philip's joke. She stares at the ground, embarrassed.

Edward introduces Penny, enthusing about the pending dance performance and Philip's comedic routine. Thomas and Margaret present themselves, sometimes to a frosty reception. Margaret greets Henry, "Hello, Nephew!"

"Hello, Aunt!" replies Henry, respectfully, "Lovely to see you again! How is my cousin, Henry Tudor?"

"Still in exile after his appointment as Henry the Sixth's successor!" retorts Margaret through gritted teeth, whispering to Henry as they enter the White Tower, "I think we should meet. There is much to discuss. Why are you aligning with Richard York when you are of Lancastrian stock and married to a Woodville? I have a proposition!"

Henry says nothing. He knows which side his bread is buttered...today! They agree to meet. Henry decides he has nothing to lose and perhaps much more to gain!

Sisters Beth and Margie lock arms and reminisce about their childhoods, recalling when baby brother Richard wet the bed! Beth enquires, "Where are you staying in London, Sister?"

"Eltham Palace," replies Margie, "on Richard's suggestion. He says our brother, Ted did some amazing things to the layout and the interiors during his reign, including an impressive library."

"We're staying at the Palace of Placentia in Greenwich," informs Beth, suggesting. "Why don't you stay with us? It's only a short boat trip away, and you won't have to be alone!"

"Are you sure John won't mind?" enquires Margie, politely, "I couldn't possibly impose."

"I won't hear another word," replies Beth, mouthing the suggestion to John, who nods his approval. "There. It's settled. You're staying with us!"

Edward leads the handwashing before sitting on his throne in the centre of the table. Uncle Richard and all the adults sit to his right while Rich and all the children sit to his left. It is better that way - everyone can chat about things they have in common! Penny rejoins Liz and her dance colleagues.

The banquet begins with repeated buffet trips as course after course flows, and stomachs serve as quantity gauges. After the third course, Edward claps, demanding silence and orders, "Send in the Royal Jester. It's time for some entertainment!"

Two waiters hold back the curtains for Philip's grand entrance. He runs through on his air shoes like a stampeding giraffe, stopping just in time to start juggling three clubs. Philip adds a fourth, then a fifth and then a sixth until he is juggling three white and three red clubs so fast that they appear pink! Everyone watches with spinning heads like washing machines set to *final rinse* until dizziness insets. It is as if Philip is trying to hypnotise the audience and escape with all the gold and silver!

Edward directs the applause as Philip collects all six clubs and jumps down from his air shoes. After *fire-eating* and *acrobatics,* Philip takes a pack of cards and walks up and down the table, magically *hiding the King* and *turning the King of Clubs into the Queen of Hearts.* The children watch in disbelief while the adults try to second guess the trick, demanding Philip to repeat several times until everyone is finally flummoxed! Penny and Liz spy through the curtains, smiling at each other as Philip appears to be entertaining.

"Jokes!" hollers Edward, "Tell everyone *the beer jokes!*"

Philip bows to the applause after delivering, "...still no eye beer!"

"More," orders Edward, echoed by everyone screaming, "More, Jester. More!" repeating as Philip delivers another punchline, "...I'm a little hoarse!"

"This is the last one!" exclaims Philip, pulling a sad face then a happy face and jiggling his hat bells, "Knock, knock..." he begins, whispering loudly behind a raised hand, "...you say, *who's there?*"

"Who's there?" everyone shouts.

"A plant!" declares Philip, whispering loudly behind a raised hand again, "...you say, *what type of a plant?*"

"What type of a plant?" everyone screams.

"A Plant-agenet King...so hold onto your heads!"

No one laughs! Penny and Liz worry that Philip has taken a step too far. Then Edward starts to giggle, repeating, "...*hold onto your heads...it's a Plantagenet King* at the door...that's funny!"

Everyone follows suit, thankfully for Philip, who makes a swift exit.

Liz accompanies the musicians into the Great hall. She announces, "Good evening, Your Highnesses, Dukes and Duchesses, Lords and Ladies...and young heirs," smiling at the children who roar their approval. "We would like to perform three dances for you. The first dance is called *Pretty in Pink.*"

Penny and the dance troupe appear from behind the curtain, skipping to the music. Six girls, dressed in white and six girls dressed in red, create two opposing circles. The *white girls* form arches under which the *red girls* pass, reversing for the *white girls* to come through *red arches* before making a larger circle of intermittent *white* and *red girls*, spinning around on the spot. The music gets faster and faster until the girls discard their red and white costumes to reveal twelve pink dresses, curtsying to the applause.

"The second dance is called *Love, Peace and Harmony*," introduces Liz.

"Amare. Pax. Concordia!" Edward translates into Latin.

Six handholding pairs dance in line, separating to loop around and come back together, repeating and reversing direction, and concluding with two lines of six standing opposite each other - one side curtsying and the other side bowing to the applause.

"The third dance is called *King Edward, the Dragon Slaying Angel!*" announces Liz, ushering out the girls to change.

The red and white scale dragon appears from behind the curtain...leaving its lair! The front dancer simulates *spitting fire* and rides a chariot-like vehicle pushed by the second girl. Wings automatically *flap* as the wheels turn. The third dancer thrashes a long sweeping tail and completes this impressive amalgamation of poetic movement and mechanical ingenuity. The audience gasps. Eight girls in pink satin dresses and waving branchlike extensions encircle the dragon hiding it from view. The music builds...

Penny appears, looking identical to Edward, wearing black velvet and sparkling in her shiny breastplate armour and halo. She dances around, swaying her sword and darting in between the *pink* trees, now pulsing and pulling out as the music reaches its crescendo.

Penny thrusts her sword into the dragon's belly to a standing ovation!

29
I hurry with Godspeed!

Penny stays with Ed and Rich and their cousins to watch the summer solstice sunset, playing Gameball until no one can see the pig's bladder ball anymore! They agree to reconvene for an early picnic breakfast and conclude the *first to eleven* - Elizabeth, Edmund and Humphrey leading Ed, Rich and Penny *eight, six!*

Disorientated by the extra-long daylight, everyone except Henry and Katherine and their young family who leave early must spend the night after missing the Tower's curfew and the Ceremony of the Keys at ten o'clock. Ed and Rich have no choice - held captive and forever under the watchful *tired* eyes of Fenton and Filbert!

The children do not mind as the alternative of moving at night-time to another Palace even makes those most determined to stay up as late as possible crack the widest yawn. The adults are oblivious, remaining in the Grand Hall and continuing the banquet through to the small hours...most consuming a trifle too much!

Penny is up early while Liz and Philip treat themselves to a lie-in after the stress of delivering the previous evening's performances. Penny exits her house wearing her blue tights and pumpkin pants - there is no way she is donning a dress to play Gameball!

"Good morning, Penny," welcomes Edmund, loud and clear across the Tower Green, trying to walk on cobbled together air shoes, declaring, "We haven't been to bed!"

"That's not true, Edmund," contradicts Elizabeth, whom everyone calls Liza to avoid confusion! "I have just woken you."

"Oh, very well, *Miss Sensible!*" rebuffs Edmund, turning red with embarrassment, "But we did sleep outside in the open all night!"

"Not *sensible*," defends Liza, calm and collected, "just *truthful!*"

"I want some of those long stick things like your father had, Penny," outlines Edmund, repeatedly falling then discarding his sticks in disgust. "He makes it look so easy!"

"Air shoes!" details Penny to curious expressions. "He's going to make me some after Edward's coronation. I'll ask him to make you a pair if you like?"

"Is a Yorkist rose white?" exclaims Edmund, rhetorically, "Of course I'd like a pair...in bright green if possible!"

"Say no more," answers Penny, smiling, "they are as good as made...in bright green!"

They lounge on a sizeable tapestry rug surrounded by various banquet leftovers and fresh breakfast items, brought out half an hour before by Cook and her assistant. Fenton and Filbert stand near the lion's cage, watching Primo, Secundus and Tertius pace up and down restlessly...almost aggressively.

"We were just talking about your father's jokes," informs Ed, offering Penny a piece of fruit and pouring her a glass of apple juice. "Where does he get them from?"

"I've *no eye deer!*" replies Penny, quick-wittedly, and taking a large bite from an overripe peach, sending a torrent of juice down her hand...forcing her to lick unceremoniously.

"I've *still no eye deer!*" shouts Humphrey, lying on his back with eyes closed and legs and arms in the air, trying his best to imitate a dead deer with no eyes. "Get it?!"

"I have no idea..." continues Rich to misplaced moans and groans, "...how he turned the *King of Clubs* into the *Queen of Hearts.*"

"Me, neither," agrees Liza, shaking her head and dripping golden honey over a chunk of bread, "or where he hid the *King.* How very perplexing!"

"What does *perplexing* mean?" enquires Humphrey, now upright and tearing slithers from a chicken drumstick.

"It means *puzzling...confusing*, Humphrey," replies Liza, enjoying being the eldest in the group.

"What do you call a camel with three humps?" Penny recollects a joke from Philip's endless supply.

"Is this a joke?" asks Rich, eager to add to his repertoire.

"Yes!" replies Penny, repeating, "What do you call a camel with three humps?"

"I don't know!" everyone responds, "What do you call a camel with three humps?"

"Hump-three!" delivers Penny, triggering endless taunts towards Humphrey.

"That's enough, boys!" scolds Liza, sensing her brother's discomfort. "No one likes being teased."

"It's just a bit of fun, Liza," clarifies Ed, confirming, "it's not as if Humphrey has three humps!"

"Unlike Uncle Richard!" ridicules Rich, mimicking Richard's stoop - everyone encouraging him with escalating laughter before stopping abruptly as Richard appears...as if by magic, standing disapprovingly beside the picnic rug!

"I came outside, children," says Richard, ignoring their tomfoolery and bowing, "Edward, Your Highness. To inform you that Sunday Mass starts shortly in St. John's Chapel. I suggest you finish breakfast and make your way over in good time."

"Where is Aunt Anne going?" enquires Ed, seeing Anne exiting the White Tower with Thomas and Margaret Stanley and head towards the main entrance.

"Anne needs to collect something from Baynard Castle, our other London residence, and has agreed to accompany Lord and Lady Stanley to Sunday Mass at St. Paul's," informs Richard, reaching down and taking an apple. "She will return soon after and join us for lunch. After which Aunt Beth, Uncle John and Aunt Margie will journey to the Palace of Placentia in Greenwich...with all you children," concludes Richard, pointing at Liza, Edmund and Humphrey before departing.

"Let's finish the game after Mass," proposes Ed to nods of approval. "It won't take long for Penny, Rich and I to whip your behinds!"

Liza, Edmund and Humphrey protest, debating the final score and which of them will strike the winning shot! Ed picks up the pig's bladder ball and wellies it down filed to collect later.

Penny watches Fenton and Filbert escort Ed and Rich, and their cousins towards the Garden Tower. She grabs a few items from the picnic buffet and wanders over to the three lions, remembering her first encounter and how it could have been her last!

"There you go, boys," Penny shouts, throwing each lion a drumstick to be devoured like a pinch of salt, "just a little snack."

Primo roars. The lions are unsettled. Something is awry. Penny cannot put her finger on it and dismisses their anxiety as an understandable distaste for captivity. She does not have to wait long before Edward, and the others tear out into the Tower Green to resume the pressing matter of Gameball!

"On the 'ead, Ed!" shouts Rich, skirting around Elizabeth to create room, screaming, "Nooowww!"

Edmund tries in vain to cover the ground to protect his goal - an empty bread basket turned sideways. It is inconsequential. No sooner does Rich's head make contact than the pig's bladder ball bursts like an exploding bubble-gum bubble, covering Rich's face in old wrinkled pink leather! Edward declares the game a draw despite Liza, Edmund and Humphrey leading *nine, seven!*

Anne rushes into the Tower Green, shouting deliriously, "Richard! Richard! Come hither!"

"What is it, my sweet?" enquires Richard, exiting the White Tower, unaware of the children simulating nausea at his sickly-sweet name-calling!

"I hurry with Godspeed from St. Paul's..." begins Anne, panting to regain her breath, "...where the Canon, Ralph Shaw..."

"...yes, I know of the Canon," interrupts Richard, uneasy with his wife's hysteria, questioning, "What of him?"

"...in his sermon," continues Anne with a simmering smile set to boil over, "he preaches the truth about Edward the Fourth and Lady Eleanor Talbot."

Edward and the children listen in disbelief as Anne describes the moment when, "The Canon declares Edward the Fourth's children as illegitimate...with no claim to the throne!" adding with uncontrolled happiness. "Giving credence to the rumours and fuelling an angry mob...marching here as we speak...to denounce Edward...and for you, Richard York...to be King...and for me...Anne Neville...to be Queen...and for *our* Edward...to be the son and heir!"

30
That's put a hammer in the works!

"Can this be true, Uncle?" Edward asks Richard, worried.

"I am sure there is some sort of a mistake, Edward," replies Richard, caught between a rock and a hard place. "Why would your father appoint me as Lord Protector in charge of your succession if he knew this indiscretion to be true?"

"Where there's smoke, Richard..." corrects Anne as her smiles and jubilations vanish momentarily, finishing, "...there's fire!"

"I shall talk with the Canon," suggests Richard, appealing to Edward, "and tell him that he is mistaken and that the rumours have been spread by Lancastrians determined to overthrow the House of York."

"But this isn't the case," points out Anne, becoming agitated with Richard's resistance, "because they are calling for you, Richard York, and brother of Edward the Fourth to be King!"

"Exactly!" shouts Henry, speed walking towards them and pointing in the direction of St. Paul's, "I've seen the demonic crowd with my own eyes, chanting and cheering in their hoards. Why would the people be marching here to denounce young Edward then call for you to be King, Richard?"

"I have no idea!" responds Richard as the children giggle at his coincidental punchline. "Perhaps they are fed up with the prospect of continuing unrest and see a *child King* as someone to perpetuate problems rather than to solve," reasons Richard, staring at the floor then heavenwards, seeking divine intervention. "You have to remember that tens of thousands have died over the past few decades. Brothers battling brothers, friends fighting friends...splitting families and breeding mistrust. No one wants *Civil War*. It's the worst kind of conflict - knowing the enemy, you kill."

"They want *you* to be King, Richard," proclaims Anne, standing in front of Richard and clutching his hands, "You, a noble soldier with an infamous track record on the battleground. A warrior to continue the Yorkist claim and continue your brother's legacy."

"And what will become of me, Uncle?" enquires Edward, feeling like a spare part and pointing at Rich, "And my brother?"

"I made an oath to God," replies Richard earnestly, "and to your father...to protect you...which I will honour. Have no fear."

"So, can Rich and I leave now?" poses Edward, excited at the thought of reuniting with his mother and sisters, "Collect our belongings and abandon the Tower?"

"Perhaps!" replies Richard, seeing Anne's look of complete horror.

"I think you should remain until after the coronation," interjects Anne, appearing to have the boys' interest at heart, "You don't want to encounter the angry mob!"

"You never know what they'll do to you!" affirms Henry, smiling at Anne, who reciprocates. "It's best to listen to your Aunt, Edward. She makes good sense!"

"What's all the commotion?" enquire Beth and John, joining and squinting in the midday sun.

"Edward isn't going to be King!" informs Liza before Richard, Anne, or Henry can answer. "Some Canon has told everyone that Uncle Edward was married before Aunt Elizabeth...so Ed and Rich have no claim to the throne!"

"Not that old rumour," dismisses Beth, exclaiming, "I won't let this continually affect the House of York. This stupid rumour has already brought about the death of Brother George, who tried to blackmail Brother Edward...to his eventual detriment!"

"I think you'll find the rumour had little to do with George's death," responds Richard, uncomfortable at opening old wounds. "George blew with the wind. One moment a Yorkist, the next a Lancastrian and then back again as a Yorkist but always trying to overthrow our brother, Edward until his final arrest for treason."

"Leaving my deceased sister's children orphaned," adds Anne, solemnly and directed at Beth and Richard.

"It seems coincidental that Bishop Stillington, the creator of this despicable rumour," condemns Beth angrily, "was an ally of Isobel...your sister...George's wife! How convenient!"

"Are we talking about Brother George who should have then married my recently deceased stepdaughter, Mary?" queries Margie, eager to join the conversation - Liza bringing her up to speed. "Goodness me!" exclaims Margie, "That's put a hammer in the works!"

"We deviate from the main issue," points out John calmly. "Whether the rumour bears substance, it has been preached as the truth and as such causes this change of circumstances."

"Hello, Anne!" shouts Margaret, entering the Tower Green, "I came as quickly as I could after dropping Thomas at home with a headache! The slightest whiff of blood, and he runs a mile!"

"Good God!" screeches Beth, turning to John, "Look what the cat's dragged back in. Your ex-wife!"

"We were *three* when we married!" exasperates John, "And we never even met before the marriage was annulled!"

"And rightly so!" disapproves Beth, "It's bad enough that Margaret then married Henry Tudor and bore her only son at fourteen! And now she's masquerading as a Yorkist with Lord Stanley!"

Penny and the children look at each other mischievously, hearing things usually withheld from young ears!

"Good afternoon, Aunt Margaret," welcomes Henry, running over to escort her and whisper. "Did you have anything to do with affairs at St. Paul's earlier?"

"Maybe!" Margaret disguises her whispers through a tight smile, adding sarcastically, "Maybe not, Nephew!"

"Is this part of your plan you want to discuss?" mutters Henry.

"Maybe!" Margaret disguises her whispers again before winking, "Maybe not, Nephew!"

The adults say little, glaring at each other with distrust, all shocked by the last twenty-four hours...arriving for the coronation of Edward, now facing the inauguration of Richard!

"Let's retire to the Grand Hall," suggests Anne, taking control and ushering in the adults before turning and instructing the children. "Stay out until we call you in for lunch. We have more to discuss."

A few moments pass before Liza breaks the ice, wincing, "I didn't see that coming!"

"Neither did I," replies Ed, crestfallen and confused, "but something tells me that there's more to this than meets the eye."

"Did you see how happy Aunt Anne was?" poses Edmund.

"She doesn't like us," states Rich, matter-of-factly. "Never has and never will!"

"Your Uncle Richard was as shocked as you, Ed," points out Penny, positively. "That's reassuring."

"Let's listen at the windows," suggests Ed, pointing to the open windows then conscious of Fenton and Filbert, adding, "subtly - as if we're seeking shade."

Ed, Rich, Penny, Liza, Edmund, and Humphrey saunter over to the first window and sit casually except Liza, who remains standing to eavesdrop, relaying, "I can hear Uncle. Richard with Mother and Father and Aunt Margie."

"What are they saying?" asks Ed, still shaken and *hit for six!*

"Mother and Margie are calming Richard and lecturing him on his responsibilities as King," informs Liza, "saying that he must distance himself from Uncle Henry and Great Aunt Margaret, both of whom believe that they have an alternative claim to the throne. Richard says nothing, but Father is trying to convince him!"

The children shuffle to the other window to find Anne, Henry and Margaret. Liza reports once more. "Aunt Anne is excited," Liza reveals, straining to hear every word. "She's asking Margaret to be her train-bearer at the coronation. Margaret accepts. Then Anne is rabbiting on about regaining all the titles and estates she once had."

"Unbelievable!" exclaims Ed. "What else?"

"Henry is saying how they need to cement Richard's succession," continues Liza, "with a meeting of Parliament this Thursday."

"That's my coronation," sulks Ed, "or rather, *was* my coronation!"

"All the Council members are in London for the coronation," continues Liza, "Henry says it's as good as in the bag! Now Margaret is offering to assist and assert her influence...and now they've disappeared!" concludes Liza, shaking her head in disbelief.

"It wreaks of a Lancastrian plot," declares Ed, joking in the face of adversity, "to put another Yorkist on the throne!"

"What are you doing down there?" questions Anne suspiciously.

"Nothing, Aunt," answers Liza, innocently and crossing her fingers!

"It's lunchtime!" announces Anne, unconvinced. "Come inside!"

159

31
Fünf. Fünf. Fünf!

Penny walks over to Primo, Secundus and Tertius after Ed and the others disappear inside for lunch. The three lions are less agitated than before.

"Are you feeling better, boys?" enquires Penny, grabbing the bars, "I think I know why you were so worked up earlier," she continues as all three lions now stare in her direction. "Your animal instinct sensed danger...that Edward was going to have his throne ripped from beneath him before he has a chance to sample!"

Tertius roars as if to say, "It's appalling!"

"I know!" replies Penny, pulling their legs, "Because you won't get to wear your pink coats!"

Penny finds her old farthing and stares at the likeness of the three lions. She spits and rubs five times, scrunching her eyes.

The magic happens once more!

"Hurry up and get changed, Penny," encourages Liz, opening the front door and requesting, "give me your judo gear, and I'll wash it for next week."

"Do you have to?" moans Penny, "It's always like cardboard after being washed!"

"I'll add some fabric softener," proposes Liz, knowing precisely what Penny means, "and I'll hang them out to dry naturally rather than use the drier!"

Penny runs upstairs to change into her England shirt. Today is Semi-finals, and England is playing its nemesis - Germany. France beat the tournament favourites, Brazil, yesterday, scoring two second-half extra-time goals to win *four, two*, and reach the Final. England is delighted that Brazil has been knocked out, but getting past Germany will be a feat in itself. Germany has beaten England on the last five occasions - twice going to penalty shootouts!

"What time is Aunty Margaret coming?" asks Penny, entering the kitchen and making a cheese and marmite sandwich, exclaiming, "I'm so hungry, Mum!" scoffing an enormous mouthful, revealing, "Judo gives me the munchies!"

"Don't fill yourself up," advises Liz, flicking through her digital photos on her camera then showing Penny. "That's a great shot of you, don't you think?" murmuring, "There will be food at the Yeoman Warders Club," eventually answering, "Margaret said she'd call when they get here, and we'll go and meet them at the front gate...anytime soon."

Aunt Margaret is Phil's elder sister. Penny cannot remember where she lives but knows that she has recently moved after remarrying recently. Her first husband died a few years back. He went into hospital for a routine operation but contracted sepsis and died twenty-four hours later, which was also devastating for Henry, Penny's cousin, now studying International Politics in Paris. Tom, Margaret's new husband, is much older, but Phil says he is *perfect* for Margaret, bringing creativity into her life! Tom paints and sculpts while Margaret submerges in legal jargon and infinite numbers as a solicitor specialising in accountancy fraud! Apparently, Margaret and Tom met when Margaret answered Tom's advertisement for life models. Penny shudders at the thought of old wrinkly bodies and posing nude...especially in front of strangers!

Liz's phone starts ringing. "It's Margaret," informs Liz, showing Penny her phone screen, answering to tell Margaret that they will be there in five minutes.

"Phil will meet us in the Yeoman Warders Club," converses Liz, escorting Margaret and Tom across the Tower Green with Penny. "He gets off at six, and the match kicks off at six forty-five."

"I don't normally follow football," admits Tom, holding Margaret's hand and looking at her fondly, "but since meeting Margaret with her obsession..."

"...hardly an obsession, darling!" interjects Margaret, joking, "When you support a team like mine!"

"...but since meeting Margaret with her *passion...*" corrects Tom, smiling at Penny, "I've come to see football in a new light."

"Who do you think's gonna win?" quizzes Penny, answering before anyone has a chance. "I think England *three, two* in full-time!"

"That's confident!" remarks Margaret, "I wish I could share your optimism!"

"C'mon, England!" cheers Liz, singing, "*Football's coming home. Three Lions on a shirt...*" revealing her England shirt.

Margaret shows her red England shirt, adding superstitiously, "This is my lucky shirt. England always wins when I wear it!"

"That's because you bought it for the World Cup, darling, and England hasn't lost a match yet!" jests Tom, unzipping his jacket to reveal a white t-shirt with a hand-painted red St. George's Cross emblazoned across the front.

The thought of *Three Lions* makes Penny think about Ed and his precarious position. She still believes that it is best to keep secret her time travels and delay any revisit until after the match!

Liz shows Margaret and Tom into the Yeoman Warders Club and a sea of red and white! Penny applies her lion mask and finds Ted and Rick near the front.

"I saved you a seat, Penny," says Ted, shuffling onto one seat then introducing his friend, "This is Klaus. He's in my class!"

"Hi, Klaus," greets Penny, discerning he is the elder brother of her classmate who gave the Germany flag for her crutches before teasing, "I see you support the losing team!"

"Yeah, yeah. Very funny!" replies Klaus with a discernible German accent, puffing out his Germany chest badge and pressing his *black eagle* mask, which squawks, *GOOOAAALLL!* Taunting, "Count the stars, Penny! One. Two. Three. Four!"

"Four stars. So, what?!" responds Penny, frivolously.

"It means Germany has won the World Cup four times," informs Rick as Klaus nods and pats the stars four times.

"Well, we're gonna beat you today," replies Penny in desperation, "and then win the Final!"

Ted lightens the mood by offering around his red and white lion chews, specially made for England's World Cup campaign and available in the Tower Gift Shop. Klaus initially rejects the offer but eventually takes four white ones – they are sweets, after all!

Penny sees Phil arrive as the national anthems begin.

The first half is full of *ooohs* and *aaahs* as England, dressed in red, fails to score, and Germany, dressed in white, near misses several times. Phil brings them refreshments at half-time. His England shirt shows signs of something spilt. "Before you say anything," anticipates Phil, glancing at Ted and Rick, "your father got overexcited and chucked a whole pint over me!"

The second half has an entirely different atmosphere. With every spent minute, the crowd becomes less and less animated, nervously biting nails and occasionally praying!

Germany gets the ball and moves up through midfield, catching the England full-back out of position. A perfectly flighted ball finds the sweet spot of the Germany striker's boot. The England goalkeeper saves, but the ball bounces forward, spinning back out of control past the scrambling keeper and into the England...*GOOOAAALLL!* Squawks Klaus - a solitary sound in a head-holding room of distraught England supporters!

There are five minutes to go. Klaus is beginning to believe, chanting, "Fünf. Fünf. Fünf!"

There are ripples of inevitability and philosophical clichés. One supporter is even crying...inconsolable and infantile!

The fourth official displays one minute of added time. Germany has the ball and is playing down the clock. The Germany *left midfield* passes the ball backwards. The England *number ten* predicts the pass and intercepts, running past the last line of defence and into the penalty box. The Germany goalkeeper has only to shadow the England striker and push him out left. Instead, he dives for the ball, misses and takes out both legs from beneath the England striker. The referee blows his whistle. Not for full-time but for a "PENALTYYYY!" the whole room explodes!

32
The great escape!

The Germany goalkeeper tries every trick in the book to distract the England *number nine*. The referee warns him, threatening a yellow card, resulting in a sending off following a previous first-half incident. The England striker ignores the shenanigans and places the ball on the penalty spot without so much as a glance at the goal or the keeper. He walks back six paces, carrying the weight of the nation on his shoulders.

The atmosphere is electric. Penny is convinced she hears a pin drop as everyone holds their breath and stays perfectly still.

The England striker turns in slow motion and runs at the ball, blasting it straight down the middle at chest height, banking on the goalkeeper diving one way or another...which he does! The ball smacks the back of the net to nationwide cheers and sighs of relief, exaggerated inside the Yeoman warders Club as decorum disintegrates into disorder temporarily.

The crowd thinks it is all over, but it is not! The goal brings another thirty minutes of scintillating and nerve-racking play, each side becoming less and less adventurous and more and more cautious as the final whistle nears. The referee blows for a *one-all* draw.

Red and white players collapse to the ground, gripping their legs or catching their breath as the relief of a draw rapidly replaces with the anxiety of a penalty shootout! Both teams congregate in the centre circle, discussing and deciding their *fateful five*. The keepers saunter to the *Germany end* after England appears to lose the toss. They shake hands in good sportsmanship.

"I can't bear it!" exclaims Liz, joining Penny at the front, "Why did we have to lose the toss!"

"We didn't, Mrs Woodville!" informs Ted as England sends its first player into *no man's land!* "We chose the Germany end so that we have the advantage of scoring first!"

"IF you score first!" remarks Klaus, pressing his mask prematurely to groans of contempt from around the room, adding smugly, "Which history says you have difficulty in doing!"

England scores in the *top left* to roaring lion masks! Germany scores in the *bottom left* to a single eagle squawk! England scores another, again *top left*. Germany scores another, this time *bottom right*. England kicks and clips the Germany keeper's gloves...and scores *right middle*. Germany shoots *right middle* and squeezes one above England as the keeper also dives right but too low! England scores again in the *top left*. Germany duplicates. It is *four, four!*

"C'mon England!" everyone screams as if their lives depended.

"C'mon, Germany!" counters Klaus, but he is unheard.

The England *number nine* places the ball. Now it is a mind game. Does he repeat his earlier penalty or change tactics? The keeper guesses incorrectly as the blasé striker blasts the ball straight down the middle again and scores. It is *five, four* to England.

The Germany end falls quiet, facing defeat or sudden death. Can their captain execute with unfaltering reliability? He shoots. The England keeper takes a chance and remains steadfast, gambling on a centre shot. It would not matter which way he went - he could have nipped to the local café for a cup of tea because the Germany captain misfires his shot sky-high, poignantly landing amongst the Germany supporters, aghast and shell-shocked!

"YEEEAAAHHHHHH!!!" erupts England, seeing its team through to the World Cup Final and building a human pyramid above its keeper! The Yeoman Warders Club chants *Football's Coming Home* led by none other than Phil and John...and Tom!

Ted and Rick console Klaus for a few moments before relishing the victory, jumping up and down and doing some sort of tribal dance! Penny hugs Liz, shouting, "We did it, Mum! We're through to the Final...and a single cockerel is no match for Three Lions!"

"That...my child!" replies Liz, sighing profoundly and with the most effusive smile Penny has ever seen, "Is what you call *the great escape!* Drawing in the last minute of full time and then Germany doing the unthinkable...and missing a penalty!"

Penny contemplates *the great escape* as Liz rejoins the others. "That's it!" Penny says to herself, decisively, "I'll help Ed and Rich escape from the Tower!" studying her farthing with *Angel Edward* standing victorious, proclaiming, "They need their own guardian angel...and that's me!"

Penny spits and rubs the coin five times, scrunching her eyes. The first attempt fails, but the second is successful.

Magic happens once more!

"So, what do you think, Penny?" enquires Ed, repeating his question, probing, "Are you with us, Penny, or, as you always say...are you away with the fairies?!"

167

"What was the question, Ed?" questions Penny, refocusing her gaze from the window towards Edward and noting Edmund, Humphrey and Liza sitting around a table in the Garden Tower chambers, "Sorry, my head was in the clouds!"

"Liza overheard Aunt Beth and Aunt Margie talking," repeats Ed, shaking his head at Penny's endless array of phrases. "Saying that Uncle Anthony, whom Uncle Richard imprisoned after intercepting us on the way to London, has now been executed along with a few other conspirators. We were discussing whether it was under the orders of Uncle Richard or Aunt Anne?"

Penny ponders, noting that Fenton and Filbert are nowhere to be seen and standing guard outside. "I think it's Richard acting on behalf of Anne!" answers Penny, elaborating, "Anne is calling the shots to send a message to the Lancastrians...not to think about toppling them as King and Queen!"

"And I've just seen Anne talking to Henry on the Tower Green," continues Liza, "on my way back from discussing potential suitors with Mother and Father and Richard."

"What do you think they were saying, Sister?" asks Edmund.

"I couldn't get close enough, but whatever they were saying," replies Liza, showing concern for Ed and Rich, "they kept looking towards the Garden Tower with a distinct look of mischief."

"I asked Mother what will happen to you, Cousin Ed and Cousin Rich," adds Humphrey, "and she said that Uncle Richard would continue to honour and protect you. Apparently, Richard may have his faults, but *dishonour* isn't one of them!"

"What if the rumours of Father's indiscretion are disproved?" poses Rich, wishfully thinking. "And we *do* have a claim to the throne?"

"That's why we can't trust Anne," answers Ed. "She is probably plotting to be rid of us once and for all!"

"I also heard Mother and Aunt Margie talking badly of Anne, Henry and Margaret," contributes Liza, suggesting, "and that they are the ones to fear!"

"We cannot take the risk," states Penny, seeing the look of despair in Ed and Rich. "We have to get you out of here!"

"Don't you think I have considered this since my arrival," says Ed, helplessly, "but there are enough guards to intervene even if we can shake Fenton and Filbert!"

"Not on the day of Richard's coronation!" points out Penny, leaning in to whisper for fear of being overheard, "All the guards will be deployed to Westminster, only leaving a skeletal contingent!"

"How do you know?" enquires Ed, bemused.

"My Ma and Pa were filling me in about the revised details for the new coronation," outlines Penny, frowning at Ed sympathetically.

"You mean, *no pink!*" declares Ed despondently.

"No pink...or air shoes!" details Penny, "and no Hannibal...but Richard's keeping the three lions!"

"Back to your idea, Penny," directs Liza, pointing out their lack of time before returning to Greenwich, demanding, "How are we going to get Ed and Rich out of here?"

"There is just over a week before the coronation on July the sixth," continues Penny. "We know that everyone will depart for Westminster the day before on the grand procession."

"Edmund, Humphrey and I will be part of the coronation," reveals Liza, "so we won't be around!"

"I am to attend as well," says Penny, "but I have a plan for the *great escape!* Come closer, and I will explain..."

33

Operation *Three Lions* is go!

The following week drags slowly for Ed and Rich, but for everyone else, it is manic! The craftsmen and women run around like blue bottom flies, complaining of the lack of time but knowing that no excuses will be tolerated! Liz and Philip are glad to be involved, fearing that Richard and Anne would dismiss them immediately following Edward's demise, now moaning and groaning at the new demands to create a different set of dance renditions and fresh jokes!

Liza, Edmund and Humphrey have been over twice, accompanying Beth and Margie on their responsibilities as the sisters of the new King. Margaret visits Anne most days, and Henry assists Richard with decision making on everything that Anne has left so kindly!

It is Saturday. The celebrations begin tomorrow. Penny heads over to the Garden Tower to finalise the plan for the Princes' escape. Fenton and Filbert, standing either side of the front entrance, cross poleaxes, shouting gruffly, "No one to enter," looking directly ahead and continuing robotically, "By order of Richard the Third!"

"It's me, Fenton...Filbert," protests Penny, pleading, "I must see the Princes!"

"They aren't Princes anymore," responds Fenton with clever clogs, "Not since they were found to be illegitimate!"

"I must see Edward and Richard!" demands Penny, appealing to Filbert's better nature, "Just for a few moments!"

"You can't!" replies Fenton at the same time as Filbert says, "You can!" both looking at each other before pulling back their poleaxes and Filbert concluding, "You can...when the King departs. He's talking with Edward and Richard as we speak."

"Why didn't you say that in the first place," remarks Penny, taking the opportunity to quiz Fenton and Filbert on their whereabouts tomorrow. "So, will you be going to the coronation?"

"We've been ordered to stay behind and guard Edward and Richard," informs Fenton, complaining, "everyone else gets to go, but we have to stay and look after two boys...who aren't even heirs anymore!"

"So, all the other guards are going to the coronation?" Penny probes further.

"Not so much *going*," responds Filbert, "as *working* at the coronation."

"As King Richard's and Queen Anne's personal Guard," adds Fenton, "alongside King Richard's army of six thousand fresh in from the north, to quash any threat or conspiracy by the Lancastrians to disrupt the coronation."

"You must be annoyed?" prompts Penny to gain more information, "Being left on your own and missing all the fun!"

"Apparently, the Duke of Buckingham is looking to relieve us straight after the coronation," continues Fenton, lowering his guard, "so we might get to enjoy some of the evening entertainment."

"Surely the Duke will be attending the evening celebrations?" questions Penny, immediately adding to appear less interested, "I hear the Duchess is expecting their child any day soon..."

"It won't be the Duke himself," explains Filbert, revealing too much, "Someone called *Sir James Tyrrell* will be coming with another..."

"...I think you're mistaken, Filbert!" interjects Fenton, realising their carelessness, concealing rather feebly, "The Duke is sending someone with *some tame squirrels* for the menagerie..." stopping abruptly as the door opens and out hurries Richard without so much as a *Hello* or a *How's your father!*

171

"In you go, Penny," instructs Fenton, glad to see the back of her and shaking his head vehemently at Filbert, "You have five minutes, and then we have to escort Edward and Richard to new chambers in the White Tower!"

"What's this about you moving to new chambers?" queries Penny, anxiously after closing the door. "This wasn't part of the plan!"

"Richard came over to tell us that he wants to move us to a safer place within the White Tower during the coronation," replies Ed, despondently, "but I know the place...it's dark and dingy by comparison."

"Fenton and Filbert say you are going there in five minutes," details Penny, wondering if their great escape has gone out of the window, declaring, "We have to bring the escape forwards."

"Why?" asks Rich, "I thought escaping under cover of darkness is safest."

"It is," Penny agrees, answering, "but apparently, someone is coming after the coronation to relieve Fenton and Filbert," she relays, adding, "someone on Henry's instructions...someone called Sir James Tyrrell with one other."

"That doesn't sound good!" remarks Ed, sensing danger, "Tyrrell is a confirmed and loyal Yorkist, but he might do anything if Henry has bribed or fed him false information!"

The door opens, and in walk, Fenton and Filbert, ushering Ed and Rich into a single line formation, then marching them to the White Tower. Penny follows!

They march through Tower Green and into the White Tower, climbing two flights to arrive into Ed's correctly described *dark and dingy* chambers. Fenton and Filbert exit, shutting the door behind...now under lock and key and imprisoning the two boys...along with Penny! No words are spoken - their faces say everything. A single window reveals a thirty-foot drop and highlights a four-poster bed and a simple table with two chairs.

"The plan to escape out of the window is no longer feasible!" points out Penny, gazing down and racking her brains for a solution.

"Even if we could get Hannibal to stand under," jokes Ed, trying to remain positive in the face of adversity. "But somehow, I think someone would spot us running away on a ten-foot elephant!"

"The main problem is how to tell Edmund and Humphrey to come earlier," sighs Penny, kneeling at the door and peering through the large lock, "regardless of how we get you out of here!"

"You should have said, Penny," remarks Rich, swallow-diving onto the bed and exclaiming, "I've never felt such a lumpy mattress!"

"What do you mean?" queries Penny, jumping onto the bed alongside.

"Aunt Beth is coming with Edmund and Humphrey this afternoon," replies Rich, to Penny's delight. "Something about bringing Father's coronation ring for Richard."

"Liza found it at Greenwich Palace," adds Ed, jumping onto the bed and also wincing at its lumpiness before pulling himself up alongside Penny and Rich.

They gaze into the four-poster bed upholstered ceiling in bewilderment. Ed begins to complain about recurring toothache while Penny starts to formulate a revised plan. Rich cries for his mother, homesick and in need of some love and affection...and reassurance.

"I've got it!" proclaims Penny, sitting bolt upright on the bed after consoling Rich with a hug. "I have a plan that should work...with a little bit of convincing acting!"

Penny explains her new plan, detailing it minute by minute and point by point. Ed and Rich's initial dismissiveness turns to acceptance, conceding that there is no alternative other than staying and encountering the fate Henry...and probably Anne, has installed! Penny puts out her hand, palm down, encouraging Ed and Rich to apply theirs, declaring, "Operation *Three Lions* is go!" lifting their conjoined hands upwards to resulting giggles.

Penny knocks on the door. Fenton unlocks the door and allows her to leave. Penny pleads with puppy eyes, "Seeing as the boys are cooped up," she points out, "they're wondering if they can play with the suits of armour we saw on the floor below?"

Fenton looks at Filbert before nodding, "I don't see any harm, but they have to play with the armour in their chamber."

"Thank you, Fenton. Thank you, Filbert," says Penny, hugging Fenton and Filbert - unaccustomed to demonstrable affection!

Fenton and Filbert escort Ed and Rich to pick out a suit of armour and return to their chambers, again under lock and key. Penny disappears downstairs to wait for Edmund and Humphrey, crossing her fingers that nothing interferes with their arrival.

She knows she has not got long before dance practice and Liz comes looking for her!

34
Let's wrestle!

"There's been a change of plan!" whispers Penny as Edmund and Humphrey arrive with Beth. "Ed and Rich have been moved," divulges Penny, pointing to the dark and dingy room in the White Tower, "and Fenton and Filbert are to be relieved by some men whom Henry is sending over after the coronation and whom we think have malicious intentions."

"I'll be five minutes," informs Beth, disappearing inside as the bellowing voice of Anne screams orders to an array of submissive servants. Edmund and Humphrey know *five minutes* means at least thirty!

"What does this mean, Penny?" asks Edmund.

"We have to bring the escape forwards," outlines Penny, upbeat, "to coincide with the time of the coronation."

"That's in the middle of the day," shrugs Humphrey. "Surely we'll be spotted?!"

"Don't worry," replies Penny, positively, "there won't be many guards. Just Fenton and Filbert and the guards at the front gate."

"So what time do you need us to arrive?" enquires Edmund, hoping Beth honours her *five minutes!*

"We need to work with the tides," replies Penny, elaborating. "Low tide is around *eleven*, and high tide is around *five*. The coronation starts around midday but will go on most of the afternoon before the evening celebrations. It's four miles from Greenwich to the Tower. Suppose you leave Greenwich around *three* that should give you plenty of time to travel with the incoming tide and arrive by *four-thirty*. Then we'll aim to leave as the tide turns, aiding our return to Greenwich with good speed."

"How do we get out of going to the coronation?" questions Humphrey, cutting to the chase.

"Tell Liza she should go," answers Penny, justifying, "so as not to raise any more suspicion than is necessary, and she can keep a lookout at Westminster..."

"...Liza will be delighted!" interrupts Edmund, smiling, "Several suitors will be there, and she thought she would miss her opportunity!"

"Whatever!" dismisses Penny, unsure why Liza is so determined to meet a suitor! "Anyway...as I was saying. Take these red and white colour sticks," continues Penny, retrieving them from her bag.

"What are they for?" puzzles Humphrey.

"You're gonna make everyone think you have the plague!" replies Penny, drawing a circular dot on the back of her hand with the white colour stick, instructing. "Paint a few of these on your body," she continues, drawing a smaller circular red dot on top of the white dot. "and say you're feeling unwell!"

"Genius!" remarks Edmund, observing the authenticity of Penny's handiwork. "No one will want to risk taking us to the coronation covered in pox!"

"How will we slip out of Greenwich Palace?" poses Humphrey, drawing his own pox mark on the back of his hand as practice.

Penny reaches into her bag and hands Edmund and Humphrey each a small white fabric sack, stitched with black facial features and woollen strands to match their hair colour...and, of course, a few red and white pox marks! "Take these and stuff them with some clothing and place them on your pillow," Penny demonstrates by pushing her hand into one of the sacks. "Put a pillow down the bed to resemble your bodies and then sneak out. You should be back by six...in time for supper...unmissed and undiscovered!"

"Even if someone discovers we are missing," rationalises Edmund, "No one will condemn us for pulling such a stunt to miss the boredom of a coronation!"

"Are you going to pretend to have the plague, Penny?" questions Humphrey, trying and failing to insert his head into his sack before stuffing it inside his jacket.

"I need something that will be bad enough to stop me from going," specifies Penny, "but not so bad as to keep my mother from attending the coronation!"

"What do you have in mind?" probes Edmund.

"Let's wrestle!" blurts Penny...out of the blue, leading Edmund to an appropriate area on Tower Green.

"Excuse me?" responds Edmund, querying, "Did you say, *Let's wrestle?*"

"I did!" answers Penny, matter-of-factly.

"I don't wrestle *girls!*" objects Edmund, looking at Humphrey and laughing.

Penny says nothing. She grabs Edmund by his jacket and pushes him back to shift his centre of gravity. Then she pulls him forwards, throwing Edmund to the ground over her protruding left leg and entrapping him beneath her as she sits on his chest!

"What was that about, *girls don't wrestle?*" teases Penny, dismounting and helping up Edmund.

"I didn't say, *girls don't wrestle!*" corrects Edmund, brushing himself down, "I said, *I don't wrestle girls!*"

"Too late!" points out Penny, smiling at Humphrey, who's astounded and delighted by her antics. "Let's wrestle!" Penny challenges Edmund once more.

"Very well, Penny," concedes Edmund, taking a stance. "Let's wrestle!"

Penny and Edmund are equally matched, unable to throw either down...now that Edmund is prepared!

"What are you doing, Edmund?" shouts Beth, exiting the White Tower, scolding, "I thought you knew better than to wrestle girls!"

Edmund has no time to answer as Penny wraps her leg around his leg and twists, pulling them both to the ground and onto their sides. Penny screams, "My ankle, Edmund!"

"Get off her, Edmund," orders Beth, coming to Penny's rescue, "Can't you see, she's hurt!"

Penny writhes around in agony, grabbing her ankle and sobbing, while Edmund tries to console her.

"Go and get a stick, Humphrey," commands Beth, helping Penny to her feet. Penny grimaces when she exerts any pressure.

"I'm really sorry!" apologises Edmund, propping up Penny.

"I should hope so, Edmund!" declares Beth, hurrying Humphrey. "Let that be a lesson!"

"What's happened?" shouts Liz, running to Penny's rescue. "Are you hurt, Penny?"

"I am!" declares Penny disappointedly. "I don't think I'll be able to dance at the coronation,"

"I don't know what came over these two," explains Beth, "but Edmund and Penny thought it sensible to wrestle!"

"Wrestle!" exasperates Liz. "Of all the stupid things, Penny!"

"It was my fault!" admits Edmund, attempting to take the blame, pleading, "Please don't be mad with Penny!"

"Luckily, we'll be able to manage without you, Penny," reasons Liz, "but you'll miss the coronation with all its pomp and ceremony."

"That's alright!" says Penny, using the stick for assistance. "I'm sure there will be others!"

"I really am sorry," Edmund whispers to Penny, worried, "Has this put the cat amongst the pigeons?"

"How do you mean, Edmund?" questions Penny, under her breath.

"Will you be able to assist Ed and Rich tomorrow?" clarifies Edmund.

"Of course, Edmund... Stupid!" mutters Penny, winking and drawing a wry smile, "It's all an act!"

"You had me fooled!" admits Edmund, helping Penny with her first steps, declaring. "How crafty are you?!"

"Right. Let's go, boys," rallies Beth, apologising to Liz once more. "We still have lots to do at home in preparation for tomorrow."

"Bye, Penny," shouts Humphrey, oblivious to Penny's convincing performance, "I really hope you get better soon!"

"Bye, Penny," yells Edmund, heading for the front gate and trying not to give the game away, "I'm sure you'll feel much better!"

"Stage *Primo* of *Operation Three Lions* is complete," Penny says to herself, "bring on tomorrow for *Secundus* and *Tertius!*"

35

Bye, Fenton. Bye, Filbert. Enjoy your evening!

The following morning sees the Tower awash with frenzy. Liz and Philip rise early - although the coronation is tomorrow, they must perform during the procession to Westminster.

"Are you sure you're going to be alright on your own?" enquires Liz, waking Penny from a deep sleep. "I've prepared enough stew to see you through today and tomorrow. We'll be back early the day after tomorrow."

"I'll be fine!" replies Penny, groggily, "Please don't worry, Ma. You go and have a great time...and dance your hearts out!"

"Doctor. Doctor." Philip begins a joke as he enters Penny's bedroom, continuing the following line, "I'm not happy that you cut my leg off!" pausing for effect and changing his voice to deliver the punchline, "Tough!" You haven't got a leg to stand on!"

"Oh, Pa!" groans Penny, delivering her own punchline, "Tough! You shouldn't have come in here *legless!*"

Liz and Philip kiss Penny goodbye, leaving Penny to contemplate two days apart. A bugle sounds the beginning of the procession a few hours later. Penny runs downstairs to view the spectacle, remembering her stick to limp outside and across Tower Green if anyone sees her. Richard and Anne sit aloft on oak thrones, each carried by six burly guardsmen. The three lions, cloaked in purple and large white Yorkist roses, roar restlessly in their gilt-covered cages. Beth and John follow behind with Liza. Penny searches for Edmund and Humphrey and breathes a sigh of relief when they are nowhere to be seen! Margie, Henry and Katherine, Margaret and Thomas follow with other dignitaries. Liz and the dance troupe move gracefully to the accompanying musicians. Philip juggles and performs acrobatics. Penny hopes they can endure the nine-mile trip to Westminster!

The Tower of London empties like its moat into the outgoing tide as the procession snakes its way out through the front gate and beyond! Only the baboons and Ursula remain with Hannibal held captive within his enclosure. Penny passes the day, preparing a bag of props, going over her plan repeatedly, and praying that everything will go like a burning candle in a still room!

The following day is like no other. An uninterrupted summer breeze swirls eerily in the Tower's enclosure. Penny discerns the faint sound of trumpets in the direction of Westminster. She waits patiently until lunchtime to launch stage *Secundus* of Operation Three Lions - to get Ed and Rich out of the Tower! She grabs her bag and strolls over to the White Tower, careful to limp as she approaches Fenton and Filbert - bored standing guard or rather *slouching guard* on two chairs summoned from another room!

"Hello, Fenton. Hello, Filbert," greets Penny as if it is any other day. "How are you today?" continuing before they have a chance to respond. "I've brought some lunch for Ed and Rich."

Fenton grumbles and unlocks the door, eager to rejoin his forty winks.

"Hi, Ed. Hi, Rich. Look at you in your armour suits," announces Penny for Fenton's benefit - her limp *vanishing* when the lock sounds. "Ready for the beginning of the rest of your life?!"

Penny helps Ed and Rich out of their armour suits to arrange them *sitting* at the table by the window.

"I can't tell you how uncomfortable they are!" declares Ed, stretching his back. "We didn't dare disrobe in case Fenton and Filbert confiscated them!"

"Two days in armour suits!" informs Rich, repeating, "Two days!"

"It'll be worth it in the end, boys," encourages Penny, opening her bag. She places the food on the table together with some twine, two spoons and several strands of pink ribbon. "Ready to embrace your feminine side?" she teases, tossing Ed and Rich each a pink satin dress - identical to the one she is wearing!

"I've always liked the idea of wearing a dress!" admits Ed, enthusiastic about dressing in drag, "And today's the day!"

Penny braids the boy's hair and ties using the pink ribbon, ensuring they all look as identical as possible. She rubs white powder into everyone's cheeks and applies some rouge. Ed and Rich practise Penny's walk with Rich standing on tiptoes to be the same height. Then Ed and Rich repeat, "Bye, Fenton. Bye, Filbert. Enjoy your evening!" over and over until they all sound the same!

Penny attaches some food to the twine and lowers it out of the window. She fixes two spoons on two different lengths and inserts them into the armour, testing by yanking the twine. The spoons jangle inside the armour as if Ed and Rich are moving around and playing chess! "Beyond genius, Penny!" proclaims Ed, "Fenton and Filbert will never know the difference!"

They eat the remaining food for sustenance and wait patiently, playing cards. Penny looks out of the window to read *four o'clock* on the makeshift sundial she made earlier - Fenton and Filbert always take turns for a break on the top of each hour. "You first, Rich," instructs Penny, giving him the thumbs up. "See you down by the Garden Tower."

Penny stands behind the door and asks to depart. Fenton opens the door. Rich tiptoes out with a limp, saying in his best *Penny* voice, "Bye, Fenton. Bye, Filbert. Enjoy your evening!"

"Filbert's not here!" points out Fenton, relocking the door. Penny and Ed hold their breath as Rich, cool as a cucumber, responds, "Bye, Fenton. Enjoy your evening!"

"Bye, Penny!" says Fenton, fidgeting and desperate for the toilet.

"Now you, Ed," says Penny, hearing Fenton scamper away on Filbert's return. She also gives him the thumbs up and repeats, "See you down by the Garden Tower."

Ed is a *natural*, mimicking Penny down to a tee. Filbert relocks the door and settles back down in his seat. Penny waits patiently, not wanting to go too soon in case Fenton and Filbert become wise and jeopardise everything! Finally, Penny asks to leave, bidding farewell to the empty armour suits! Adding, "Bye, Fenton. Bye, Filbert. Enjoy your evening!" limping away.

"Hang on a minute!" puzzles Filbert, "I just let you out!"

Penny freezes, replying and relying on Filbert's less than quick recall, "You must have dreamt it, Filbert!"

Fenton opens the door to see Ed and Rich playing chess in armour suits - the spoons jangling away as the birds peck away at the food below! "She's right, Filbert," says Fenton, locking the door and gesturing for Penny to go before mocking Filbert, "You've been snoring like a true Lancastrian...all day!"

Penny finds Ed and Rich down by the Garden Tower, hiding in the rose bushes. She recounts her near-miss while Rich and Ed enjoy swishing and swirling their long dresses - especially Ed!

"Halt. Who comes near?" Penny whispers into the dark tunnel moat exit, affectionately known as *Traitor's Gate*. There is no answer. The tide laps the walls and threatens to spill over at its peak. "Halt. Who comes near?" Penny whispers again.

"*Three Lions*," Edmund gives the password, which echoes inside the tunnel. "Ready to roar!"

Penny, Ed and Rich climb aboard the rowboat as Edmund and Humphrey tease Ed and Rich about their attire. Ed retorts, "You should try it, Edmund. I know for a fact, you'd like it!"

"Enough, boys!" reprimands Penny, afraid that Fenton and Filbert will appear at any moment.

"Enough, girls!" continues Edmund to Penny's disapproving stare.

"Now it's stage *Tertius* of Operation Three Lions," briefs Penny, pointing towards Greenwich, "to get Ed and Rich to safety and the hidden confines of Aunt Margie's ship!"

"Ready to sail for France," excites Ed, smiling at Rich and tasting freedom for the first time in months. "To settle in Burgundy with Aunt Margie until it's safe for our return."

Edmund rows with the outgoing tide. Penny has an idea to go faster. "Each grab an oar, boys," she orders, "and rather than row, paddle like this," demonstrating the dragon boat technique, "and stroke to my beat," banging the boat like a Viking slave's galley.

The Tower disappears as they round the bend for Greenwich, catching sight of Margie's ship and chanting to Penny's beat,

"Primo
Secundus
Tertius.
Roaring
Soaring...
Bolting!
Primo
Secundus
Tertius!"

36
Gripp and Rocky!

Edmund resumes rowing duties and steers gently towards Margie's galleon, anchored alongside the Palace of Placentia. Approaching riverside, Penny grabs a dangling rope to steady the rowboat while, one by one, Humphrey, Edmund, Rich and Ed disembark, using the rope ladder Edmund had lowered a few days before.

Ed turns to Penny as he puts his foot on the first rung and smiles, saying, "Thank you, Penny," reaching into his pocket. "I hope our paths cross again soon. Please take this as a token of my gratitude and to remember me!" Ed hands Penny the gold farthing sample the Mint Master had given, stating, "Like you, it's one of a kind! All the others will be melted and reissued with Richard's ugly mug!"

"Thank you, Ed," says Penny, staring at the farthing and trying not to become emotional. "And, Ed..." she begins as Ed glances down for the last time, "...perhaps you should change your name! Give yourself a new identity...something original!"

"I've always fancied *Perkin* or *Warbeck!*" replies Ed, smiling then disappearing inside the ship in his pink satin dress and braids.

Penny sits for a while, delighted that Operation Three Lions is a success. "I better be heading home," she says to herself, turning over Ed's gold farthing to show Three Lions, glinting in the early evening sun. She spits, rubs five times and scrunches her eyes to no avail. Penny takes out her magical farthing and places it next to the shiny farthing. This time she spits on her worn coin, rubs *three lions* five times and scrunches her eyes.

Magic happens once more!

"Look at this, Penny," says Liz, studying a photo on her camera screen. "I was just showing Margaret and Tom the photos from the judo competition when I saw this!"

Penny studies the photo of herself, Ted and Rick standing outside the White Tower just before they head for the water bus.

"Look in the second-floor window," directs Liz, zooming in. "There are two ghostly figures in pink dresses!"

"It's just a trick of the light," suggests Penny, studying the apparitions of Ed and Rich behind Ted and Rick.

"I thought that, too," says Liz, studying the image again, "but they look so real!"

"Perhaps they're the *Princes in the Tower!*" quips Penny.

"In pink dresses?" dismisses Liz, closing her camera, "I hardly think so! Probably just tourists!"

Penny smiles to herself, thinking, "If only she knew!"

"Let's go!" rallies Phil, clapping his hands excitedly. "Chop, chop. The match starts in thirty minutes!"

Phil and Liz escort Margaret and Tom to the match. Penny follows, remembering her lion mask at the last moment. John and Beth, and Ted and Rick are waiting outside so that everyone can walk together. Phil had said that the Tower was laying on something spectacular for the World Cup Final, and he was right!

The White Tower north face is draped in a large white full-width widescreen. Rows of rapidly filling chairs fill the space between the Crown Jewels and the White Tower.

"How's the ankle, Penny?" enquires Dr Burgundy, genuinely.

"Much better, thank you, Doctor," replies Penny, rotating her ankle as proof.

"And how are the braces, Penny?" enquires the dentist, pointing at his own mouth for verification.

"I'm getting used to them, Mr York," Penny smiles to show her England coloured braces...everyone chanting *C'mon England!*

"Hey, Phil...Liz," announces the dentist, beaming and holding out his assistant's hand to show her sparkling diamond, "Anne and I are engaged!"

"That's wonderful, Richard," respond Phil and Liz, shaking his hand. "Congratulations!"

"Mr Hastings!" shouts Liz, waving. "Over here."

Will Hastings arrives with Henry *Duke* Buckingham and his wife Katherine - heavily pregnant and looking as if she is about to pop!

"Thank you for inviting us," says Henry, patting Katherine's belly. "We managed to offload the youngsters with the grandparents. I hope you don't mind, but I invited three of my students - brothers, Eddy and Humphrey and their elder sister, Liza!"

"Absolutely not!" replies Liz, proposing, "Why don't you children go with Penny and Ted and Rick to the front?"

Penny and Humphrey and Ted and Eddy recall their contests while Liza stares nonchalantly, searching for children her age!

Fenton and Filbert have swapped their work overalls for England shirts and painted their faces in the St. George's Cross.

The children sit in the front row and acquire two more lion masks for Eddy and Humphry. Liza would not be seen dead in one!

The whole of the second row is full of clucking cockerels! The local French school is invited to cheer on France, all wearing golden cockerel masks, crowing *BUUUTTT* in a French accent! Which to all the England supporters sounds more like booing!

The projectors are switched on. The whole audience is flabbergasted as the World Cup Final broadcasts in 3D. Some of the children run to the screen, attempting to touch the players, much to the amusement of the adults!

Everyone stands and sings the national anthems. The whole country bellows *God Save The Queen*, and *La Marseillaise* travels across the Channel to do battle!

England plays in white, France in blue. After the furore of the Semi-final and England progressing on penalties, the Final is dull by comparison. Neither team wants to make mistakes, playing defensively and unimaginatively. Crowds up and down the country and outside the White Tower scream advice and tactical manoeuvres, but England does not hear…nor does France!

Just as it looks like the match is going to extra time and certain penalties, the England *number nine* collects a floated pass from the right-back, spins on a sixpence and shoots the ball in the direction of the French goal. It swerves one way and then the next, and then as if by magic and good fortune rather than by design, the ball goes beyond the outstretched fingers of the diving keeper and into the top right corner. GOOOAAALLL!

England wins the World Cup!

And the whole of England erupts into incredulous chanting of *Three Lions on a shirt…years and years of hurt!*

Car horns and champagne corks resonate nationwide!

On hearing *Three lions*, Penny needs to know if Ed and Rich make it to France. Amongst the commotion, she finds her worn coin and holds it in her palm. She spits, scrunches her eyes, and just as she begins to rub, Phil comes from behind and lifts her, hugging and jumping up and down in jubilation. The coin flies out of her hand and high into the air. Penny watches in slow motion as the coin lands on a drain, spinning temporarily until it topples, never to be seen again. Penny searches in vain, full of sadness and frustration that she will never be able to travel back-and-forth or catch up with Ed and the boys ever again.

As she prepares for bed, Penny takes off her shorts. Out of the left pocket rolls a shiny gold farthing. She picks it up and studies both sides. It is Ed's gold farthing - the one he gave her when climbing aboard Margie's galleon.

"Goodness me," exclaims Penny, spitting on the angel and rubbing, "who needs a worn-out farthing when you can have a shiny new one!"

Unfortunately, there is no *turning inside out* or *travelling back*. There is no *magic* as Penny opens her eyes to find that she is still standing in her bedroom, preparing for bed!

"I'll never know what happened to the Princes in the Tower!" acknowledges Penny, remembering, "No one knows for sure, but at least I know in my mind that I helped them to escape!"

Penny stands in her nightdress, brushing her hair half-heartedly and talking to herself in the mirror. "No one will believe me if I tell them about the magic farthing," she surmises, smiling. "No one that is...except for Gripp and Rocky!"

CAST

The players!

The Present		1483	
Penny Woodville	Schoolgirl	Penny Woodville	Dancer
Phil Woodville	Chief Yeoman	Philip Woodville	Jester
Liz Woodville	Attendant	Liz Woodville	Dance Teacher
Ted Suffolk	Schoolboy	Edward York	Edward the Fifth
Rick Suffolk	Schoolboy	Richard York	Duke of York
John Suffolk	Yeoman	John de la Pole	Duke of Suffolk
Beth Suffolk	Guide	Elizabeth York	Duchess of Suffolk
Eddy	Judo student	Edmund de la Pole	Princes' Cousin
Humphrey	Judo student	Humphrey de la Pole	Princes' Cousin
Liza	Judo student	Elizabeth de la Pole	Princes' Cousin
Will Hastings	Judo Coach	William Hastings	Baron Hastings
Henry Buckingham	Judo Coach	Henry Stafford	Duke of Buckingham
Kathy Buckingham	Housewife	Katherine Stafford	Duchess of Buckingham
Margaret Burgundy	Doctor	Margaret York	Duchess of Burgundy
Richard York	Dentist	Richard York	Duke of Gloucester
			Richard the Third
Anne Neville	Dental Assistant	Anne Neville	Duchess of Gloucester
			Queen Consort
Margaret Stanley	Penny's Aunt	Margaret Beaufort	Lady Stanley
Tom Stanley	Penny's Uncle	Thomas Stanley	Lord Stanley
Fenton & Filbert	Tower Workmen	Fenton & Filbert	Princes' Guardsmen

THANK YOU FOR READING

I HOPE YOU ENJOYED AS MUCH AS I ENJOYED WRITING

PENNY AND THE FARTHING

GAVIN THOMSON

BOOKS BY GAVIN THOMSON

JOANNA AND THE PIANO

ISAAC AND NEWTON'S APPLES

PENNY AND THE FARTHING

THE WARS OF THE ROSES

TWINNING TALES SHORT STORIES

MMXIX

II

Printed in Great Britain
by Amazon

17168201R00112